Jenna,

Hey, thanks for being great.

I hope the book finds you well and you enjoy it.

Nick
Desjardin

In-Between Days
by Nick Desjardins

© Copyright 2017 Nick Desjardins

ISBN 978-1-63393-502-0

Published by

◤ köehlerbooks ™

210 60th Street
Virginia Beach, VA 23451
800–435–4811
www.koehlerbooks.com

In-Between Days

by
NICK DESJARDINS

VIRGINIA BEACH
CAPE CHARLES

For Hurricane J,
The storm that changed everything.

1

In the twelve years I've been here, I had never once been late—until today. Sleep was almost nonexistent here. A little over a decade of next-to-no rest, yet somehow, on the day I was getting out, I managed to get eight full hours. That was the kind of ironic meal this place served up, but today was the last time I'd have to swallow it.

I rolled out of bed and looked at the answering machine, flashing red and beeping incessantly. Sighing, I smacked the button next to the blinking light and listened as a gravelly croak crackled out of the tiny box.

"Owen, this is a courtesy reminder of your appointment with Michael this afternoon concerning your release. Remember to have your things packed, your affairs in order, and please arrive early." Her tone somehow managed to be both acrid and apathetic, the true sign of a hardened receptionist.

"Yeah, thanks for that," I muttered, my tongue pressing hard against the back of my teeth. I pulled on my only good pair of jeans, doing my best to look presentable. I stared into the wall mirror, dirty and cracked since long before I took up residence here. There were bags under my eyes. Everyone here had them.

It took me a minute or two to find a shirt, another five to locate my wallet, and an embarrassing amount of time to tug on a pair of boots. Emerging from my apartment building, I almost expected to be greeted by a bright, colorful day, as if the universe knew I was on my way out, but that wasn't the case. Every ounce of pigmentation that should have been there—the blinding yellow of the sun, the pristine white clouds, the deep and comforting blue—had been swallowed up by an unforgiving, ravenous gray. It was always gray here.

Boot heels clicking on the sidewalk, I ran to the bus stop, shoving keys and other belongings into my pockets along the way. I made it to the corner just as the bus door closed. Smacking against the side as it began to pull off, I managed to catch the attention of the driver. Begrudgingly, he hit the brakes and pulled the lever.

"Most people know how to make it to the bus stop on time," he sneered, his words slightly muffled by the plush growth above his upper lip.

"And most people prefer a nice 'hello there' as a greeting." I shot a smile, my best attempt at a courteous "fuck you," as I dropped change into the coin slot. I took the seat behind him and, for what I hoped would be the last time, observed the marks on his neck. The rope had burned a perfect red ring all the way around—a grotesque ascot to match his flared slacks and seventies-machismo mustache.

Looking at my forearms, focusing on my scars for what must have been the hundred-thousandth time, I knew I had no room to judge him. The scars hadn't faded from that dark pink shade in twelve years. Though no one ever said anything about them,

I couldn't help the urge to hide them. The guys in charge always said that once I left, the scars would leave too. None of us knew if that was true. No one who left ever came back. Why the hell would they?

I caught his glare in the rearview mirror and rolled my eyes. After today, I'd be done with his scowls and shrugs. I settled into my seat—non-cushioned and comfortless, solid steel covered in cracked faux-leather. The bus chugged along to the next stop, squealing and groaning on the uneven pavement.

Though I hated this place more than I'd hated anything in my entire existence, I had stopped the self-pity and wondering what I'd done to deserve it all.

The commute was especially bad right now, and it seemed to get longer each day—Greek heroes had shorter journeys than this. Some days it rained, and some days the sun was blinding, peeking out of the clouds like a cosmic game of hide-and-seek. But the color never changed. You'd go crazy in a place like this if all you ever did was stare up at the great big monochrome. You learned to look at the people instead.

An old woman frequented the back of the bus, her face weathered with wrinkles. She wore a head scarf, but not as a fashion statement or cultural icon. Instead, it covered up a nickel-sized pink scar on the front of her neck, and another slightly larger scar on the back. I assumed she'd been some kind of KGB spy, and that she'd run one of those secret numbers stations. She probably turned a gun on herself when the Berlin Wall came tumbling down, distraught at the collapse of her nation and the frivolity of her life's work

A young girl with frizzy blonde braids sat two seats in front of her. She had scars like mine: big, brutal lines stretching the length of her forearms, though hers were far less jagged. They'd been sliced long before mine and she'd been staring at them long before I got here, but every time I saw them I had the urge to grab bandages and wrap her up in a blanket. She seemed so young, but I guess I had been too. I wondered why she was still here. I wondered if she ever thought the same of me.

Some people looked completely normal, and they were the biggest puzzles. It was easy to see how the ones with the obvious scars ended up here, but the others kept you guessing. It became the most interesting way to fill the time, wondering to yourself if the man in the pressed suit and slacks was here because he ruined a half-dozen marriages with acts of infidelity. Or, maybe he was one of those Wall Street guys who flew to second-world countries to fleece money or resources. Horrible thoughts, for sure, but no worse than being out in the real world, sitting on a bus passing superficial judgements.

In all likelihood, most of them weren't guilty of some spiritual crime or cardinal sin. Michael had explained it to me. For the most part, people ended up here because they weren't particularly good or bad. Those kinds of people didn't stick around for too long.

If you ran out of people to judge before you reached your destination, you were effectively left with nothing to do but count the number of scratches on the seat in front of you until the bus finally made it to your desired gray brick building. The first few years of this dismal commute were fine; there were enough people to guess about. I'd spend the whole ride dreaming up scenarios and life stories. The scarred young girl, with her long legs and slender build, had chased her dreams and tried out for the New York City Ballet. She was passed over twice, and in an act of desolation, she took a piece of a broken mirror to both wrists.

And that asshole bus driver, with his awful white, flared chinos and feathered hair, had been a happily married man with a secret lover on the side. When his wife found him in bed with his paramour, another man, he hung himself out of shame. His suicide left him scarred and driving this bus. That happened long before I was born.

Two blocks from the city, the bus screeched to a halt to let on a businessman in a sharp suit. His hair was coiffed perfectly to the side, his suit pressed and clean. He hadn't been here long, and the sneer he gave the bus driver suggested that his attitude adjustment would take decades.

"I don't have change, pal," he spat at the bus driver, adjusting his cufflinks in a threatening manner. They looked like little white sleeping pills, the kind I'd once taken far too many of. "Just let me ride to the office, and I'll pay you on the ride back."

"Look," the bus driver retorted, his words slightly garbled under his mustache, "you're holding up the route. These people have places to be, and it's *poli-shee*. Nobody rides for free. You either pay the fare, or you get off the *bushh*."

The man looked as if his stock investment plan had just been panned. He glared at the driver, a long and angry scowl focused down a large, pointed nose. For a moment, I thought he might take a swing. Though I was no friend of the bus driver, I didn't have time for a bus brawl between a couple of roughneck idiots. I was on my way to being paroled. I fished out the correct coins from my pocket and sprang toward the box, staring the businessman right in the eyes as I dropped each piece of silver into the slot.

"Sit." *Plink.*

"Down." *Plink.*

"Asshole." *Plink.*

He looked at me like I'd put three coins directly into his ass rather than paying his bus fare, defensively adjusting his sleeping-pill cufflinks as if that would intimidate me into rescinding my comment. But it wouldn't. I stared back, my callous eyes and curled lip acting as proverbial middle fingers. He got the hint, his coattails tucked between his legs as he skulked back to an empty seat next to the Russian woman. I was willing to fight him if he bothered her, but I'd done well enough to control my impulses up to this point.

The last two city blocks passed by in a rush of annoyance, adrenaline, and anxiety. My legs shook, each of them to a separate beat. One I was certain was a Ramones song I hadn't heard in years; the other was the uneasy cadence of fear. I wondered what my father might say if he were here. I hoped he'd never be here, never see a place like this. I couldn't begin to imagine what I'd say to him. *Sorry* was the only word that came to mind, but I didn't have the time to spiral into those depths.

The bus sputtered to a halt, the door hissing open. We filed out, one by one, the carnivorous gray seeping down into the city from somewhere up above, washing over and muting everything. The absence left everyone wanting, wracking their brains for far-off memories of blue skies, of a life replete with vibrancy, and of childhood—of opening up a new box of crayons, filled with more colors than you thought you'd ever need.

* * *

The courthouse, St. Peter's, was center city. Or at least it felt like the center. Except for the gray wash, it seemed entirely out of place, an archaic temple in the middle of a vast urban jungle. It was the only place in the city that never seemed to slow down, but it was too governmental to call a heart, perhaps a kidney. Floods of people were always rolling in—lifers looking to pay off debts, the freshly arrived not knowing what to expect, and the people who were lucky enough to be leaving—all climbing the granite steps to those heavy oak doors. It was too much like a church for any real comfort, but I guess they planned it that way.

Some people never made it past the statue. They'd stare up in shock at St. Peter towering over them, as if they'd stumbled onto the set of *Attack of the Fifty-Foot Saint*. I'd been here long enough to take in every crack in his marble beard, the precise angle of the tipping scales hanging from his fist. Awe faded into admiration, which quickly dissolved into apathy. I just wanted out. I was ready to go, and salvation was waiting for me in a cramped office behind those doors.

I'd never made it up the steps that quickly before, and I stood at the top like a conquering champion, ready to strap on boxing gloves with a bad eighties anthem stuck in my head. Before today, every tug at that door handle was like pulling frantically at a block of lead. But today I felt like Superman as they flew open with a simple pull. This place was as happy to see me go as I was to be leaving.

"Excuse me, pal," said an unfamiliar, sharply-dressed man as he brushed past me. He didn't even look my way or wait for me to respond, and I found myself dodging his wings as they stretched out. They pulled him up into the air, and he began spouting directions to the organized chaos below him.

"Alright, newbies, please follow me toward annex C, so we can get you documented." His voice trailed off as he led a group of confused looking newcomers.

"The hell is this place?" came a voice from behind me.

"Are those . . . Is that guy fucking flying?!"

"Don't say those kinds of things in the presence of an angel!"

"Annex B is off limits due to a wallpaper-related issue, please get a clean-up squad in here immediately," yelled another important looking man with wings. Curiosity almost got the best of me, but before I could ask questions, he rushed in the opposite direction. It was dizzying trying to navigate the bureaucratic bedlam.

"New arrivals please consult your transition manager and quickly filter into your designated waiting rooms," an unseen individual boomed over the loudspeaker. There was something unsettling about the delivery. That voice didn't come from anything resembling a human, and it seemed taboo just to hear it.

My first day here had not been easy. Dazed, distressed, staring around the great sprawling lobby, I was crammed in the middle of a group of other disoriented pilgrims, and then herded along to a waiting room by a man in khakis—with wings. That's what got most of the new arrivals; it wasn't that they were seemingly alive and well in some undefined afterlife, that their wounds were no longer bleeding and had miraculously scarred over, or even that color seemed to be a thing of the past. No, it was the feathered appendages sprouting from the back of anyone with a sense of authority.

When you know you've died, and you realize that you're still somehow conscious and existing, how can you think of questioning anyone with a divine presence? These winged beings shouted and pointed, and we followed along like cattle. With a supernatural sense of order and direction, the angels divided up the confused masses into separate waiting rooms, where we were instructed to take a number and entertain ourselves until we were summoned.

That had been ages ago, and I'd been filled with first-day-of-afterlife jitters. Today, however, I wove through crowds with confidence, ducking and dodging in between the old-timers and newcomers alike, determined to make my way to Waiting Room 13. The astonishment I felt for the lobby had long since faded, the biweekly appointments dulling the luster of anything marvelous.

The wings were now commonplace. The voice of the Metatron over the loud speaker? More akin to droning radio pop tunes than a member of the celestial choir. Visiting saints got more eye rolls than adulation. Miracles were fascinating the first time, but after a hundred or so, they were no more interesting than pulling on a pair of matching socks back in the real world, which actually would have been a miracle worth celebrating if it happened here. Before, making up stories about new arrivals helped stave off my boredom. You could always tell the new ones by the overstated looks of awe and confusion, and occasionally disappointment. But today, I wasn't intrigued by the new group walking through the heavy oak doors—not the old men, the guy in the chaps and cowboy hat, the guy dressed as a clown, not even that gorgeous blonde in front. I opened the door into the waiting room, knowing the only thing standing between me and everlasting salvation was Michael and a bunch of miserable, gray people.

* * *

When I walked into Waiting Room 13 for the very first time, no one wanted to talk. But then again, what do you say in the modernized waiting room of some ethereal realm? You're lucky enough to stare at your shoes with any sort of concentration, let alone cobble together a simple "So what are you here for? And for that matter, where are we?"

We all sat in silence, save for the click-clacking of keys behind the desk. The secretary attached to the keys seemed familiar, the same wretched receptionist you'd see a couple dozen times a year—homely and outdated, with a bored, lackluster expression and a nameplate that was criminally under-polished. She was absolutely normal. Except for the wings. I wondered how many times I was going to experience that thought as I sat waiting her to call my number.

It seemed like hours passed, maybe even a day, but without a clock it was hard to gauge. I was busy staring around the room, trying to comprehend all of this—what exactly was going on, and how I was walking and talking as if nothing had happened. Janice, the secretary, snapped me to attention. Her voice was more akin to broken china than anything else; I couldn't believe I'd managed to ignore it until then. She stared right at me, leering expectantly as she croaked out "thirty-seven?" I had to look down twice at the ticket in my hand before I finally stood and shambled embarrassingly toward the door she was guarding.

"Down the hall. To the left," she wheezed, motioning at the door. "Don't open the one on the right, and don't keep him waiting."

"Hey, can you tell me exactly where I—"

"Michael will answer your questions," she'd rasped. She didn't even bother to look at me; she was too focused on filling in the squares of a crossword puzzle. Every subsequent biweekly meeting was the same. At least today would end differently, and I had far fewer questions.

* * *

Like the scenery, the staffing, and pretty much everything here, the waiting room hadn't changed during my twelve-year stay. Janice slung me her trademark look of brooding indifference and nodded toward the ticket dispenser in the corner.

"Ticket," she mumbled. I strolled toward the machine for the last time and triumphantly wrenched a ticket loose. *Eighty-six*.

"Damnit," I muttered. Two dozen angry glares radiated heat on the back of my neck. I took a seat in the corner, surrounded by empty chairs and away from the crowd. I saw the same faces I'd seen at previous appointments. The old Russian woman from the bus was sitting in the opposite corner, and I couldn't help but wonder why we'd never spoken. I had the urge to apologize for that, to ask for her life story. I wanted to know why she was always so quiet, what she'd been doing here, how long she'd been here, why she felt it necessary to put the barrel of a gun to her throat and pull the trigger. Or if she'd even been the one to do it.

It didn't matter now. Going over, sitting down, making friends—it was pointless. As soon as I made it through this queue of people, I was on my way out. I tucked the urge away and pulled a weathered paperback from my back pocket. I started thumbing through *The Great Gatsby*, trying to remember every word that had been blacked out in some poet-hack's poor attempt at creativity, or maybe just as another one of those cruel jokes they liked to play here.

I ended up lost on West Egg at a grand party, occasionally interrupted by Janice's hoarse voice croaking out "next" or "numbah twenny-three where arh you?!" I'd peek up from the jazz age to find that the crowd had changed, new faces replacing old ones. The cattle rustler from the lobby, in full chaps and with a thick mustache, was now in the old Russian woman's seat. I had no idea if I'd ever see her again and felt a tiny bit wistful. Perhaps Michael had given her the same good news I was expecting. I wondered if we'd meet on the other side, and if she'd still carry the scars or if they'd be washed away in the transition. Would she still be wearing her grubby overcoat and that headscarf? Surely not. As far as I knew, we'd all be wearing white robes and plucking golden harps, but then again, the guys with the wings were plainclothes like us. Maybe the great Kingdom wasn't so different from this place? I just hoped my shoes would stay tied, the books wouldn't be half blacked out, and I'd never have to see a shade of gray again. I wasn't asking for much.

For a moment, I was scared—truly, legitimately, shaking-in-my-boots scared down to my soul, the kind of fear that makes itself evident on your brow and palms. What if I hated it? This gray city had been home for twelve years, or at least as much of a home as a place like this could ever be, and suddenly I wasn't sure if I could leave it behind for something entirely unknown. Sure, given the nature of my future destination, it had to be better than this, but I'd learned to live with every inconvenience this place was built on. I had even come to love my horrible little apartment, with its cracked bathroom mirror and window, the gas stove that never seemed to heat anything to the proper temperature, and the floorboards that creaked and moaned no matter how you stepped on them.

Anxiety creeped in through the cracks, and I plunged my hand into my pocket to find my lighter. I pulled the scratched-up chrome square from my pocket and clicked the lid open and shut, trying to soothe my nerves, a habit that I'd carried over from life. It seemed natural to be nervous, but I couldn't comprehend why. This was what I wanted. It was what I'd been hoping on for twelve years, what I was promised when I got here. Something . . . well, something better. I flicked the lid back and forth, occasionally stopping to fidget with the flint wheel and watch the flame flicker to life. I dragged my hand across it, wondering if maybe the feeling would start to come back, but the flame was like a ghost, and I passed right through. I stared at it long enough to get lost. Nerves placated, mind made up, I returned the beat-up firebox to my front pocket and opened the paperback again.

By the time Janice squawked "eighty-fou-ah," I'd closed the book for what I believed would be the last time, and settled in to prepare for whatever Michael could possibly ask me. Yes, I'd filled out all the paperwork. Yes, my one bag was packed. Yes, I'd snuck him a pack of smokes and I didn't care if he smoked every single one down to the filter as we talked. Yes, I was certain that I was ready to move on. Yes, I thought I'd become a better person during the duration of my stay. I looked to the left to see if Janice was ready to call the next person.

I hadn't noticed that the seat next to me was now occupied.

2

There are moments in your life that stand out above the rest, moments that mark the clear path the rest of your existence will take. When they boil down all the facts, anecdotes, half-truths and stories, these are the bullet points they give to schoolchildren—if you were somehow important enough to make it into the history books. The afterlife wasn't so different, except no one was interested in reading history books here.

Big, bold, and bright. She was a bullet point.

She was sitting next to me—the blonde from the earlier sea of new arrivals, tapping her ticket against her thigh. She'd pulled the number ahead of mine. Normally, I'd have been frustrated at the luck, but I felt a quiet calm I couldn't explain. From far away, in the infinite expanse of the lobby, she'd been absolutely eye-catching. But up close, she was incredible—the kind of exciting I hadn't seen in twelve years.

"Excuse me."

She looked at me and I could have died all over again. For so long, every single color had been on mute. Surrounded by a gray sky, every shade and hue in this place had been monochromatically muzzled. Bland grass. Bland buildings. Bland sunset. Without any real color, the days had become shallow. But her eyes. They were the kind of blue you needed to dive into, as deep as you could, where surfacing seemed like a sin. I sat awestruck, staring like some dumb, thirsty ape into pools of ice water.

"Excuse me."

Sorry, out for a swim, be back never.

"Excuse me."

She'd spoken at least twice, but I was so lost it could've been a dozen times. I was reticent to climb out of the water and back into that waiting room. The way her hair fell on her shoulders, the fit of her frayed blue jeans, everything about her was fine art. I'd seen nothing but half-assed watercolor bowls of fruit and a giant statue of St. Peter for as long as I could remember. She was the whole Louvre crammed into a tattered Thin Lizzy T-shirt and denim. I was determined to cobble together a response, a proper introduction, something that would make her forget that I was staring at her like a mental patient in desperate need of sedation.

"Y . . . yes?" My palms were sweating, a sensation I'd long forgotten and now found extremely uncomfortable.

"Do you happen to know how to get out of here?"

I had sympathy for her; being here for any great length of time could be soul-crushing. I felt the all-consuming urge to help her.

"They get lighter," I muttered, like some lost puppy. That was the best I could do.

"What?" She tilted her head with a small smile of confusion, those pools beckoning me for another long swim.

"Oh. Sorry. Your eyes; they lighten up around the outside." I wiped my wet palms against my gray jeans. "The blue, it's a real deep blue at the center, but on the outside, it lightens up. It almost gets green. That's not the best hello I've ever given, I'm very sorry." The words leaked out in a steady stream and I did my best to cover up the crack.

"Um, thanks, I guess?" She smiled politely. "And hello." She extended a hand and I shook it eagerly, completely disregarding my sweaty palm. She didn't seem to mind, but I felt like a fool as our hands pulled away.

"Could you maybe tell me how to get the hell out of here?" Her question came out as a laugh, but there was a hint of a desperation in her tone. I was too busy looking at the ticket in her hands.

"You pulled *eighty-five*," I said. I pointed at the scrap of paper she was still tapping against her thigh. Maybe I'd lost all of my people skills when I died, or left them floating during the swim. Either way, I didn't imagine I was making a great first impression.

"What?" She looked down. "Oh. Yeah, I guess I did. Is that bad?"

"No, no, it's just funny how this place works. I pulled *eighty-six* before you walked in," I shrugged. She turned her body toward mine and grabbed my ticket for her own confirmation.

"You were sitting down before me, though! Shouldn't you tell someone?" She seemed genuinely outraged, and I stifled a smile. I wondered how long that sort of intense emotion would stay with her. "Regardless, let's get back to that original point. You look like you don't want to be here either," she said. "What if we walked out right now, in protest? What's the worst they could do?"

"Yeah." I rubbed at my scalp, trying not to blush at the thought of a daring escape with this beautiful girl. I nodded towards Janice. The secretary sat behind her desk, open-mouth chewing her gum. "You can probably tell by her demeanor that our protest won't matter much. Besides, that's just how things work around here." I shrugged again, pulling my leg up into the chair and turning a little closer.

"Here?" She looked around the room, taking in what little sights there were. She seemed thoroughly unimpressed by the afterlife.

"Yeah, surely you know where you are. I mean, you know what's happened, right?"

"Of course," she laughed. "I went to Catholic school. I just really thought there'd be more fire."

My thoughts were racing. Why on Earth would this girl assume she'd been cast into the pit? What could she have possibly done that would cause her to think she was in line for an eternity of torture, or whatever it was that happened down there? I chalked it up to naiveté. I thought I was going to Hell too when I was sitting in this waiting room the first time. I'm sure the old Russian woman assumed the same—when you have no real understanding of the afterlife, it's easy to be afraid.

"You think this is Hell? I guess you're in for good news. You're not there, and barring a total freak-out or some serious rampage on your part, you never will be." That wasn't necessarily true. I'd been here long enough to know that sometimes, if you rubbed one of the higher-ups the wrong way, paperwork went missing, department names got smudged. Sure, you might have snagged the last seat on the bus, but if you were the one responsible for Raphael having to stand out in the rain and wait for a cab, it wasn't unheard of for your file to get a big red "IRREPARABLE" stamped across it, and for you to wake up to official documentation on your impending move to the inferno. It wasn't a perfect system, but I wasn't about to drop all the little quirks and idiosyncrasies of this afterlife on her, not on day one.

"Well, then," she said, surveying the room for the typical holy accoutrements, "if I can be completely honest, Heaven doesn't quite live up to hype. Don't get me wrong, I'm okay with not carrying around a harp everywhere I go, and white's not really my best color but . . ." She gave me a smile that finally pulled my attention away from her eyes. It was big, and unlike mine, it was open-mouthed, teeth beaming at the prospect that she'd beaten the system. It straddled the fine line between charming and obnoxious, and I never wanted it to end.

"Hate to bring you down, but you're not quite up in the clouds either." Like a jackass, I pissed all over her parade.

"Oh!" She looked around the room, her hopes crashing hard against the atmosphere. It was impressive how quickly she bounced back. "So, is there an elevator somewhere? There's a pretty famous song about a stairway. I'm going to be honest, this place doesn't seem like it's for me. You wanna catch a ride?"

I watched her take it all in—the dismal hues, the scowls and looks of disinterest, the bullet scar peeking out from the old Russian woman's scarf as she re-entered the room from the hallway leading to Michael's office. The girl noticed the gaudy, fifties art-deco wallpaper growing out of the corner. Her eyes fixed on the long, jagged scars crawling up my forearms from wrist to elbow. As she dropped my ticket back into my hand, she inched her slender fingers toward the scar tissue. Our eyes met one more time, and as her fingertips almost found the jagged pink peaks, I wanted to jump into one of those lagoons and never surface. Instead, I jerked my arms inward.

"What happ–"

"EIGHTY-FO-IVE!" Janice shrieked, more like a car horn than a being that might have come from up in the clouds. It was the only time I'd ever been grateful for that hideous croak; it saved me the embarrassment of explanation. The girl gave me a look somewhere between sympathy and curiosity as she rose to her feet and marched toward the door. She flashed her ticket at the slug-woman receptionist, offering me one last over-the-shoulder glance.

"Good luck!" I called to her. Though I thought I caught a glimpse of that smile from before, I don't think she heard me over the receptionist's hoarse cry of "Down the hall to the left. Michael's office. DON'T GO TO THE RIGHT!"

Her hips swung as she entered the hall and contemplated the door to the right before settling on the left. As she disappeared, so did the vibrancy she'd brought with her. I was again in a colorless world, the muted ferns and grayed hardwood floors turning knots in my stomach. I had the urge to barrel past Janice, burst down the hallway and barge straight into Michael's office. I'd throw him the pack of smokes and he'd be content to open his window and burn a few cigarettes while I marveled at the first color I'd seen in far too many years. Or he'd pull out the big red rubber stamp from his desk, my file from his cabinet, and impart a big, wet "IRREPARABLE" across my papers. I was supposed to get out today. I wasn't willing to risk his finicky temper and high temperatures for the rest of eternity.

So I stayed in my seat. It was all inconsequential at this point. When she came out of the office, she'd know everything. She'd know how this place works, she'd know how long her projected sentence was, and she'd have a job. When I emerged from the office, I'd be on my way to the clouds—if there even were clouds—and we'd just be strangers again. I was never going to learn another thing about her. It would all be some ephemeral moment we forgot about over time.

That's what I told myself, but at the same time, I wasn't sure I could handle that. I felt tethered, certain that this was some kind of soulmate stuff, straight out of an old paperback. I had to know.

* * *

I waited in oblivion for what felt like days, as though time had decelerated in some final act of annoyance. I could almost hear the Metatron whispering in my ear, "Sorry, but we've slowed time down to a crawl so you can think about how breathtaking she was and how your chances of seeing her again, though not impossible, are effectively zero. Thank you. The Management."

Time managed to catch back up the moment I heard the office door open. Before that awful croak could fill the air, I was up and on my feet. I practically met her at the door, taking her all in. I wanted—no, needed—to know everything: how many freckles dotted her pale face, where she got that ratty Thin Lizzy shirt, why she smelled like the sea. I wanted to jump right back into the arctic basins of her glassy eyes and freeze in time. When she finally got out of this place, they would drag me along with her, to thaw at Heaven's gate. I could live with that decision. They'd have fresh towels up there.

"Oh . . . hey. I guess it's your turn, right?" She seemed surprised to see me, which was fair, because I was a complete stranger who had spent an embarrassing amount of time staring into her eyes, and like a lunatic, I'd leapt to my feet to greet her. But she was smiling, and I was sure that had to count for something.

"Eighty-sex," Janice croaked. I could feel each individual blood cell racing through every single vein, my skin on fire with anxiety. My time was running out, and I was about to be relegated to a passing memory of her first day in the In-Between. I made a desperate Hail Mary.

"There's a bowling alley on Sullivan. Across from the train tracks. The Depot. If you want to talk later—"

"Eighty-sex!" Janice was both a dutiful receptionist and a horrible demon from Hell whose entire purpose was to ruin everything.

"You'll be there?" The girl seemed genuinely interested, her tone warming with her question. My temperature rose as my grasp on language began to slip away, my tongue working itself into intricate and impressive knots.

"Yeah—I—well—will. Yeah. Definitely, yeah." I was doing this. My mind was made up. I could fight the system. Just a hierarchy of angels and the Almighty. Not a tall order at all.

"EIGHTY-SEX!" Janice cawed like a full murder of crows. A vein above her left eye bulged, knocking her awful frames off kilter. I hated her more than I thought possible. I wondered if that would go on my record, if Michael would bring it up when I sat down in front of him. Surely he'd just laugh it off.

"Alright, alright, I'm going. Keep the bees in the hive," I snarled, looking at the ghastly excuse for a hairdo glued to her slug-like head.

She shot me a look that could've killed if I weren't already dead, and I volleyed back a middle finger I'm sure she was used to seeing. Then it hit me, a sudden freight train of realization concerning my complete inability to function as a human being. I hadn't even introduced myself.

"I'm Owen!" I called to her with a smile. It wasn't information anyone else in the waiting room cared about, but I hoped it would matter to her. I didn't get a chance or the opportunity to confirm. The door to the waiting room clicked shut, and with it the last hint of sea breeze left the room.

The cattle rustler waved. "I'm Steve!"

As I stumbled down the hallway to Michael's office, my excitement and anger yielded to complete terror. Every floorboard creak sent concentrated lightning spiraling up my spine. I had never been this audacious in life, let alone the afterlife. Or at least, I hadn't been for some time. I was about to march into the Archangel's office and tell his high holiness that he could take his everlasting redemption and stuff it—for a little while at least. He'd ask me why and I'd make up something clever on the fly. If I simply said "Mike, you have to let me stay, there's this girl," he'd laugh his wings off. He'd sputter, coughing cigarette smoke, and tell me to grab my bags and get to the train. But if I could convince him I wasn't ready, he'd be more inclined to let me stay and suffer a little longer. My hands quaked as I reached for the doorknob, rattling the tarnished brass ball as I twisted.

3

Michael was sitting at his desk, rigid and statue-like, gazing at the entryway as if God himself might walk through the door at any moment and plop down to fill the chair in front of him. When he saw it was me, he smiled wide, rolling up his sleeves and kicking his feet up on his desk.

"Owennnnn! Alright, I was dying for a smoke."

I pulled the pack of cigarettes from my pocket and flung them at his waiting hand. Like a well-oiled machine, he caught them, packed his smokes, ripped open the cellophane wrap, and placed one between his chapped lips. With a snap of his fingers, the dry brown tobacco at the tip turned into a bright red cherry. One deep hit left the whole room with the unmistakable stench that I'd come to associate him with.

"Lucy taught me that, y'know? Long time ago, before all the bullshit happened."

I would be impressed if I hadn't seen it a thousand times

before, though I'd have eaten that cigarette before I even contemplated telling him that. This had been our routine for years. Michael promised to try and expedite my sentence if I played cigarette courier, muttering about some "bullshit law" barring angels from purchasing certain vices in "lesser planes of existence."

"I'm surprised he lets you call him Lucy," I murmured, my mind elsewhere.

"Yeah well, he ain't got much choice all the way down there, does he?" Mike laughed at his own non-joke, his suspenders taut, struggling to contain the Archangel's deep belly laugh until it fizzled out into a smoker's cough. He reached into his top drawer and removed a golden platter, placing it on his desk. The thing was gaudy and ornate, ancient rulers dancing around the edges, surrounded by some archaic script—Aramaic, I guessed. Michael wasted no time ashing his cigarette into it, smothering and suffocating the little golden kings of yore. Divine power at its finest. He took a long, deep pull before looking me up and down, exhaling his smoke with a big smile.

"I'm telling you, kid, the smokes you got down here kick the shit out of what we've got upstairs." He pulled the cigarette back and examined it, turning it over in his fingers before resting it again between his lips. "We don't have none of the bad shit in 'em up there. But it's the bad shit that makes 'em worthwhile, you know what I mean?" He laughed, a slight cough sneaking its way in between ha-ha's.

"So?"

"So, sound more excited, kiddo," he interrupted, sounding more Mafioso than messenger of God. "You're bustin' out today, remember? You get to mosey on down to that train station, let 'em punch your card, and by the end of the night, you can be sitting up in the clouds drinking Gin Rickeys with Marilyn Monroe and Jayne Mansfield. And kid, lemme tell you, that is where you want to be. There's lots of beautiful things to see up there, but those are a sight you'll never forget."

I looked off, ignoring the crude breast gesture he made with his hands, and studying the office that hadn't changed a bit since I'd first been there. The walls were lined with photographs, all amateurishly framed, of Michael with various celebrities—sitting poolside with Elvis Presley, handing a book to Martin Luther King Jr., smoking a cigar with Winston Churchill.

"Right about that . . ." I fidgeted with the lighter inside my pocket, flicking the lid open and closed, the muffled clicks timing up surprisingly well with the rapid beating in my chest as my eyes darted around the room. In the pictures, he was missing his wings, and I always wondered just when they'd been taken, and who'd been behind the camera lens.

"Yeah! About that, did you see the tits on the girl before you? I'm tellin' you Owen, she'll be causing car wrecks while she's here, and when traffic moves at a crawl, you know that's a mighty impressive feat."

He held his hands out in front of his chest, like before, and I did my best to focus on the trail of smoke coming from between his pointer and middle fingers. Blood pumped into my fists as I clenched them around my knees. My scars throbbed and my thoughts raced. What gave him the right? What would happen if you punched an angel? Shit, what was I doing? This was Michael. The Archangel. Calm down! I leaned forward, letting my fingers relax.

"Mike. What if I'm not ready yet?" I spat the words onto his desk like spoiled milk. I didn't have to try to be convincing; my leg was shaking fast enough for the heel of my boot to pound out a breakbeat. Eye contact was impossible during this act of rebellion, even in this familiar place I only found a modicum of comfort. The tops of his filing cabinets were coated with the same thick layer of dust as day one. Strangely, his bookshelf was absolutely spotless, everything organized and tucked away. It seemed out of place. This was an office put together without any knowledge of interior design, more film-noir than *feng shui* form.

"Not ready for what?" Michael raised his eyebrows. He lowered his feet to the floor, set his cigarette on the rim of the antique platter, and brought his elbows to the edge of the desk. Then he pressed his fingertips together and stared. I couldn't tell if this was an attempt to size me up or to make me piss myself. I did my best to control my bladder. With a snap of his fingers, the filing cabinet behind me sprang open. My personal file flew high over my head and onto the desk between us. His eyes shot down to the plain manila packet, my name written in red in the right-hand corner. Clearing his throat, he brought his gaze back to me and repeated himself.

"Not ready for what, kid?"

"To go," I blurted, pressing my heel down hard into the floor to stop the restless shaking. Even after twelve years of biweekly meetings and a friendly rapport, he was still capable of intimidation with a simple look and change of tone. Breathing became a herculean task, my lungs screaming and straining to get their fill. Michael pinched his thumb and forefinger to the bridge of his wide nose, closing his eyes.

"It's just jitters," he said. "You get used to this place, and then suddenly you're afraid to leave. Happens to the best of 'em. Buck up, champ. You did your time, you learned your lesson. You're not half as impulsive as you used to be."

"No way, Mike," I said. "I'm not ready to go."

"Twelve years, kid. You've been here twelve years," he sighed. "You ain't sliced yourself open again, you never once tried to make a deal with the devil. You only tried the one time to get out of here. You don't get in fights anymore. It took you a little time, but now you're practically a model citizen. You're reformed, bud. Two weeks ago, I couldn't get you to shut the hell up about getting out of here, and now you want to stay?"

"I just don't think I've made up for everything yet. Oh! And I almost got into a fight on the bus," I lied.

"Key word, kid. Almost." He looked at me, stupefied, and took a long drag off his cigarette, turning nearly a quarter of it to ash. His free hand flipped through the file, stopping on the last page: *STATEMENT OF RELEASE.*

His swooping signature was scrawled at the bottom.

"Kid, I already signed the papers. You're in the system. Can you imagine the amount of work I'd have to do to keep you here now? Not a chance. You're goin'."

I looked at him, defeated. My stomach was falling away, as if I hadn't eaten for weeks and a giant had wrapped his hands around it to squeeze the empty contents out. All I could do was lean back in my seat and sigh, resigning to myself to the promised Paradise.

"Her name was Mia, by the way." Smirking, he leaned back too, resting his shined loafers once more on the corner of his desk. He pulled another cigarette from the pack, lighting it with another snap as it touched his lips.

"Who?"

"Thin Lizzy shirt—great band by the way—nice tits. Walked in here before you. Pale skin, glassy blue eyes, blonde hair. Kind of smelled like she just walked out of the ocean. You've been sitting there this entire time with her on your mind, except for that brief moment you's thinkin' about punching me in the face." He stretched out his wings, his smirk now a smug smile, knocking a potted plant off kilter in the process.

"W—w—wait what!? The girl who was in here before me!? I hardly even noticed her."

"Oh yeah, that girl you hardly noticed. The same one you asked to meet you at the bowling alley tonight. Gonna be a hard engagement to keep with you in a passenger car on your way to the Pearly Gates, don't you think?"

"Fuck," I sighed. "How do you even know that?"

"Really, kid?" He laughed, sucking down smoke. "Do I look like a total schmuck? I'm not some joker sittin' across from you here. I knew what you were gonna say before you said it." He stubbed his cigarette out on some ancient Babylonian's face and pulled another from the pack. "Lighter?"

"Are you sure?" I reached into my front pocket.

"Just kiddin'," he said, cigarette clamped in the side of his mouth, his finger pointed at me like a pistol. With a quick snap, the smoke began to trail again. "Love doin' that," he chuckle-coughed.

"O, lemme tell you, I think this is a piss-poor decision. You're acting on impulse. There's nothing good here. Can't get a good beer, can't watch a damn movie all the way through, can't even get an honest slice of pizza. You realize it's so much better in Paradise, right? There are plenty of girls up there too. Cleopatra's up there. You're a pretty alright looking kid. Get rid of those scars and maybe you can woo yourself a Pharaoh."

I wasn't worried about wooing a Pharaoh. I didn't care if Michael thought I had a chance with Catherine the Great, Rita Hayworth, or Audrey Hepburn. I'd seen the pictures; I'd read the books. These were women I knew, even though we'd never met. I had met Mia, yet I knew nothing about her. I had to be at that bowling alley tonight. I was empty and starving and convinced she was the only way to get my fill.

"I know this is a last-minute decision. And it's clearly not something I've even remotely thought through. But give me a couple of days. I'm not asking for some kind of permanent residence here. I know that'd be insanity. But just a few days. Let me get to know her. Please?"

Michael shrugged, ashing again into the golden platter. Lifting his head to look me in the eyes, he inhaled deeply.

"I get it kid. She's the drink that slurred your speech. 'Course you can stay. I knew you were gonna ask before you walked in." He exhaled. "I'll fudge the paperwork. Say you had a brief relapse. That'll buy you two weeks. Any longer 'n that and we're gonna have to work out some real shady shit that'll probably burn both our asses."

"So what do I do?" I tried to contain my excitement.

"You get the fuck out of my office for starters. You find your happy ass a way to work, and you tell Jonas that you aren't leaving yet. You figure out what you're doing, and you have a game plan when you walk back in here in two weeks."

"I can do that!" My thoughts were in a manic rush of plans and ideas.

"And the next time you're sitting in that chair, I expect you to tell me how she stacks up to Marilyn." He coughed his way into a laugh.

As he pointed toward the door, it swung open, muffling the string of curse words I flung in his direction. He leaned forward, his gut pulling at his white button-up, the buttons stressing and straining to keep all that holy body fat in, and extended his hand to me. Our hands met in firm, fervent agreement. I'd be back in two weeks, and even now I was wondering what I'd have to say, what trials I'd have to endure to stay longer. In the grand scheme of things, I was getting ahead of myself. Just that morning I'd leapt out of bed at the thought of a long train ride, and plush seats in a carriage with an eventual stop at the Pearly Gates. Now I was putting liberation on hold.

As our hands parted, a searing pain shot up the ridges on my arms. The worst part was how familiar it felt. I couldn't look down. I knew the jagged peaks had split open like some agonizing earthquake on the surface of my skin, and I tilted my head back, closing my eyes to hold in the tears. My mouth was locked half-agape in an effort not to scream out, and Michael looked at me ruefully. It was the first time I'd seen his tough-guy shtick waver.

"Sorry kid. I gotta have something to put on the paperwork. They'll close back up. It'll be fine the minute you walk out the door."

4

I walked all the way to Sullivan Street rather than face the bus driver, his grotesque rope-burn ascot, and the curious eyes of my fellow passengers. I needed time to collect my thoughts, or at least that's what I told myself. I wanted to stare at the train through the chain-link fence. If it hadn't been for impulse, I might be on the other side. I rubbed at my forearms the entire time, grateful that the jagged peaks had returned to normal.

The station looked almost as regal as the courthouse, and was nearly as busy. It was the only way in and out of the In-Between, and the train never seemed to be at rest for long. It would arrive in the mornings, storming in through great clouds of steam, whistling to let the angels know fresh meat was coming. The recently departed who hadn't managed to make it upstairs or down below stepped off onto the gray, splintered wood of the platform. They'd be bum-rushed by winged men with important-looking hats and name tags, who were eager to hustle the new arrivals into buses headed toward the courthouse.

In the evening, the train would sit with its doors open. If you looked close enough, you could see color peeking out through the graywash—beautiful crimson with gold accents, *Charon* painted in an elegant font on the boiler. It hadn't seemed so beautiful coming in, but with the thought of leaving in my future, it was nothing short of magnificent. Those lucky souls who'd done their time would crowd in through the turnstiles to get primo seating on the overnight trip up above, trampling over one another and any unlucky divine presence that might be in the way.

* * *

My first year here, I jumped the fence. I couldn't stand the great big dismal for one more miserable day. I'd planned it out perfectly. I ran straight through traffic like I was in a bad action movie, crossing the pavement with reckless abandon and total commitment. With a great leap, I ascended the fence, monkeying up like it was second nature, tumbling down the other side with as much grace as a hood-rat could muster. Standing. Staring. Fifty yards from freedom. I broke into a dead sprint. This was not sport, this was salvation, and every stride hit hard enough to pack the gravel beneath my boots. They might as well have given me the gold medal in escape. I'd have crawled across naked if I had to.

Two angels wearing constable helmets and nasty looks managed to grab me, and within an hour, I was sitting in Michael's office. It was late in the evening, and he made it clear that he'd rather have every single feather slowly plucked from his wings while listening to disco than be sitting in his office after hours. He mentioned something about a cocktail party with some beat poets, and though I wanted to pump him for information, I sat in child-like silence as he scolded me.

"Irresponsible. Immature. Infantile. We're giving you a second chance here! To be a better person, to learn what you missed out there in the living world. Instead, you get all churlish and try to take the easy way out." He snarled at my recalcitrance. "You're too damn impulsive, how do you not get that? I gave you all the tools, all the rules." He pulled a cigarette out of his breast pocket and lit it before continuing to admonish me. "I practically gave your little punk ass written instructions. Curb your impulses, think before you act, do your time, get out of here."

He'd seemed much thinner then, his hair slicked back, his white shirt well-tailored. All I could do was nod as he rattled on about the chance I was being given, and cringe when he threatened to send me straight down into the abyss if I was caught trying to sneak out again. Then he went in for an awkward hug, patting me on the back. It was confusing, and I was unsure where to place my hands. I didn't want to touch his wings, certain they'd be at least as greasy as his hair.

"I like you, kid," he said. "You got spunk." It was a nice sentiment, but I felt even more helpless, especially when I found out I'd added another two years to my stay. One year of this place had turned my stomach, as if it were lined with ulcers, already reminding me far too much of what I'd left behind. If this was what I was condemned to, the experience wasn't worth it. Ten years was enough to inspire a mighty, crushing sense of dread; another two was extra weight on top. When I got out of here—if I got out of here—I'd be paper-thin.

Eleven years had passed since then, but the urge to escape never did. Perhaps it was inherent to everyone stuck In-Between. You couldn't look at the train without an insatiable feeling of longing. They say everything gets better, but that's a bitter pill to swallow when you're wallowing in shit. When you can see the proof—look at that train and know that Paradise, whatever it might be, is only a journey down the tracks—you start to believe, if only a little. The tiniest shred of hope can carry you through any darkness; it was the loss of hope that got me here.

* * *

I dipped along the uneven path of the sidewalk, hopping over gashes in the pavement that were never going to be fixed. Sullivan Street was close to the tracks; you could always hear the train, even through constant traffic congestion. The impatient drivers would honk, yelling and cursing, never getting anywhere, but they did nothing to drown out the sound of the steam-whistle signaling new arrivals, or the heartbreaking *chug-a-chug* of the train leaving without you.

Jonas had named the bowling alley "The Depot" because of the proximity. Even if they didn't care to bowl a few frames, people stopped in for a last drink before they departed—one last taste of beer that even the hardest alcoholic in the middle of an Oktoberfest bender wouldn't touch.

The neon sign flickered and fizzled; it showed a miniature facsimile of Charon dragging the bowling alley's name behind it as it hurtled toward a pyramid of pins. In its better days, the sign was a sight to see, but today the wheels remained unlit and the train still. The weathered wooden door swung inward with a gentle push, and I stepped into the closest thing I had to a home.

It was dim, dingy, and deteriorated everywhere you looked. The lanes were scuffed, the balls mostly cracked, the scorekeeping monitors covered in a permanent film that was some unholy mixture of dust and dried beer. The tables in the café area were uneven, none of the chairs matched, and the booths were all worn patch-work, half-stuffed and uninviting. Jonas stood behind the café counter, his white hair gleaming in the dim light, endlessly wiping at glasses that would never be clean or sit straight. I cleared my throat.

"Owen," he cried, "*Was machst du hier?*" Jonas's head jerked with such force, I expected his crooked spectacles to fly off his sharp nose and crash onto the carpet in front of me.

"They said I wasn't ready to leave yet, J. The good news is, you aren't getting new help any time soon." I grinned at the old man. The wrinkles around the corner of his mouth deepened with his smile.

"*Ach*, you have a very poor definition of good news," he laughed, his accent thick in his throat. "And also of *help*. You make a terrible liar as well. You can tell me what really happened while you wash up the dishes." He tossed an apron at me with surprising force for his age before hobbling through the swinging wooden doors behind the counter. I was happy to get a little more time with him. Our tearful goodbye the evening before had been nothing short of excruciating.

Jonas told me on my second day that he'd been here longer than he cared to admit, that he had seen many souls do their time In-Between by working here at the bowling alley, and that he was certain he'd see many more before he hung up his apron for good. I could never understand why. His demeanor was always pleasant, especially for folks around here. He apologized to patrons for the cracks in the bowling balls, for the poor quality of the ingredients in the kitchen, and for how pin number nine on lane three never seemed to fall, even when hit head-on. He introduced himself to everyone perched on a stool or willing to bowl a game or two, ready to ask them how the afterlife was treating them that day. He may have been the only person I'd met in this place who took pride in his assigned role, as if he'd built the Depot from the ground up and resigned himself to a quiet, eternal existence in the In-Between.

He was the first one to explain to me that aging was a thing of the past, something only the living experience. I was lucky, he said, to have died young enough to still do physical labor. It should have come across as insensitive, but the old man always had an air of empathy about him, and never ill intent. He told me he was just as lucky, because he died old enough not to have to worry about physical labor, and discovered the wisdom of delegation in his old age. Naturally, he told me this while I struggled to carry a freshly filled keg into the disheveled wreck of a kitchen. It was hard to believe that a man of his character could end up in a place like this. I understood my station every time I looked at my forearms, but he had to be some sort of accident. He'd taken the time to explain in detail what he'd done, the horrible tragedies he'd been a part of, and why he deserved this place. I never wanted to believe any of it; he was too kind. Despite his own objections, I believed him to be a good man.

"And hey, before you come back here, play that 'Piña Colada' song, would you?" he called over the sound of running water.

Alright. He had his faults.

I shuffled across the scuffed hardwood floors toward the ancient jukebox in the corner. It was an art-deco antique with all the bells and whistles, shined chrome, and neon-tube lighting. It had been a gift to Jonas from St. Cecilia herself. He swore up and down that in the old days she visited all the time, but she'd since made herself scarce. From far away, it was pristine—the kind of piece you'd expect to see in a museum or some throwback film, maybe with Henry Winkler's back and boot leaning against it.

It seemed entirely out of place until you looked at the song list. Every selection was mislabeled. Certain songs had been attributed to the wrong artist, some were titled incorrectly, others entirely blank. I'd made a hobby of selecting the blank tracks and listing them on a clipboard in case I found a hidden gem, but the clipboard had a habit of disappearing for weeks at a time. Jonas was particularly fond of one of the mislabeled songs, and for over a decade my workday had begun with the frustrated pressing of K, 1, and 3. The first notes would filter out of the static-laden speakers, and like some clockwork doll, Jonas would tap his toes and start moving around like a much younger man.

Today was no different. I tapped K-1-3 without even looking, reluctantly humming along to Rupert Holmes' "Escape." I knew every word, every soft guitar rift, every snare drum beat and cymbal splash. I hated every note of it. Sometimes I thought this place might really be hell.

"Why didn't you just name this place O'Malley's?" I called back to Jonas.

"I had not heard the song before I was gifted this place!" was his reply.

I met him in the kitchen, huddled over the sink, scrubbing thoughtlessly at dishes that never came clean, in hazy dishwater that hardly passed for sanitary. His shabby penny loafers squeaked across the floor to the last notes of the song. For a man doing time, he was in the highest of spirits. I took my place beside him at the sink, dropping glasses and plates into the murk, scratching and scraping at them with a sponge that was well past its prime. Jonas freed his shriveled hands from the sink and found solace for them in a nearby dishtowel. One lanky, wrinkled finger pressed against the glass of his spectacles, nudging them higher up his nose and leaving a single, greasy smudge.

He turned to me and extended a hand. I filled it with a cleaned plate, and he *tsk-tsk*ed as he struggled to dry and wipe away the water spots, though he knew it was futile. "No shortcuts even in death," he always told me. Eventually, he accepted that the plate was as clean as it was ever going to be. He placed it on the rack with a sigh and motioned for another. This routine ran like clockwork for nearly half an hour, accompanied only by the audible fuzz and muffled songs emanating from the jukebox and Jonas's disappointed exhalations. I stared into the sink the entire time. I couldn't see my pruning hands in the cloudy water. I didn't watch my supervisor, his tireless effort to clean the dishes, or his foot tapping along with the music.

I didn't see the glass, still slick from the grimy dishwater, slip from my hands and shatter against the tiles. I wouldn't have noticed if not for Jonas's rapid-fire German profanity. My hands leapt from the grime as I rushed to the corner and grabbed the broom, eager to sweep the shards up and away so that he wouldn't hurt himself.

"So then, are you going to work in silence all day, or are you going to tell me about her?" He fixed his eyes on me, his pupils strong and sharp, even behind the greasy fingerprints on his lenses. My fingers shot to my brow to wipe away the sweat and the "Lovesick Fool" apparently written there.

"How does everyone keep figuring that out?" I crouched down to sweep the last of the pub glass's remnants into the dust pan. Jonas just smiled.

"*Alte Füchse gehen schwer in die Falle.*"

"Damnit, you can't go spouting off German proverbs. What the hell do you even mean?" I demanded from the floor.

"Old foxes understand a trap, Owen. I am not easily fooled," he chuckled. "I knew the moment you walked in. There was no disappointment on your face as you told me you are staying. Everyone is disappointed to be staying here. Even the angels look upon this place with *Verachtung*. They can come and go as they please, they just muddle through their workdays here. But you smile, the kind of smile that only a woman can give a man. I have felt that smile."

I stared, confounded by his intuition, by how everyone around me seemed to read me like a child's paperback book.

"Okay. Yes, J, there was a girl at St. Pete's today." I turned to dispose of the glass in a full bin I was certain I'd just emptied, but I could still feel his eyes, magnified by his spectacles and focusing hard on my back like those of a parent expecting an explanation. I almost heard what he said before he said it.

"There are girls at St. Peter's every day. Try that again, but with more honesty this time."

I leaned the broom back against the wall, hanging the dustpan on the hook above it. Burrowing my hands into my pockets for comfort, I stared up at the ceiling for a moment before blurting out my day like a first grader at show-and-tell.

"She was in my waiting room. Fresh off the train. She's got these eyes. They're bright, and bold, and blue—so blue. You can actually see the color!" I pushed my hair back as my emotions exploded. "You can fucking see them, Jonas, even through the gray. You get lost in them, you don't want to come back, just like the ocean. She's beautiful. And pale. She was wearing this awesome Thin Lizzy shirt and she smelled like the sea. She's got this smile, and it's the brightest thing I've ever seen." I paused to catch my breath, the entire scene replaying in my mind. "And I think she's coming here. Tonight."

He motioned me to come with him as he darted back into the café with a speed that always caught me off guard. I grabbed the tray of glasses and followed through the swinging door, depositing the tray on a shelf underneath the counter. He headed for the jukebox, adjusting a rack of bowling shoes on the way, and began pressing buttons and tapping through selections. Resting against the side of the machine, he turned back to me.

"Does she have a name, this sea girl?"

"Mia," I sighed, liked some horrible teenager in a John Hughes movie.

"That is a beautiful name." He smiled. "Does she have *Narben*?" He motioned to my arms.

I froze, nearly knocking another glass to the tile. Had there been scars? Surely I would have noticed a shocking streak of pink marring her pallid complexion.

"I didn't see any, no. I don't think that's why she's here. I think it might have been something natural, or some sort of accident."

"Michael did not tell you?" He seemed surprised as he tapped the play button—his favorite tune, again—and I filled the soda fountain with a fresh bucket of ice.

"No, of course not. I think that might be a breach of ethics."

"Good. He should not share those kinds of things. He cannot be trusted. He's a schmuck." He pointed directly at my chest, as if his ancient finger were an arrow delivering a message.

"Michael's not a schmuck!" I walked over to the taps to pull him a pint of something nameless and golden. "Besides, I don't think you're supposed to call an Archangel a schmuck. That might be why you're still here, old timer."

"I am here by choice," he said. "I have never once called Gabriel a schmuck. He follows the rules. He does not make us take numbers, he does not miss our scheduled appointments. He advises. He does not ask me to sneak cigarettes to him. He is a good man."

Jonas paused to sip from his glass, grimacing before the alcohol even touched his lips. He'd spent years adjusting to the poor quality, but no matter how many times you drank it, it never got any better. "Michael, though, he is a schmuck. Through and through."

* * *

The ancient door I'd walked through a thousand times swung wide open before either of us could say another word. I whipped my gaze from the old man to the dim, gray daylight filtering in. I knew it couldn't be her. There was no way. Nobody got used to this place in twenty-four hours. Nobody went wandering off to some strange bowling alley to meet a guy they hardly knew—not in real life and certainly not here In-Between. And yet, my gut told me to keep my eyes on that door.

I stood rubbing the same glass with the same rag, over and over, fixated on the crowd wandering in. A couple of regulars first: the guys from the bookstore down the street who'd formed a league, an angel looking to blow off some steam. The door creaked closed, and then that movement slowly reversed.

As it inched open again, my heart began pounding a fevered cadence. I had forgotten what it was like to be that nervous, every cell in my body rushing manically back and forth, desperately trying to escape. My gut told me it was her, that vibrant new shred of humanity that I'd seen just hours before. Even Jonas twisted his stool around to get a good look.

My gut was wrong; guts did not relay facts. It was the fucking bus driver, walking into the bowling alley in the most hideous leisure suit I'd ever seen. He didn't even smile or wave at me for keeping his route on time. He didn't order a drink or try to bowl a frame; he'd just stopped in to take a piss. This place never ceased to disappoint.

5

Three full days passed before I saw Mia again. Dozens of wayward souls crossed the Depot threshold each night, but not a single one was her. With every set of pins reracked or pair of shoes rented out, my decision began to weigh on me. What the hell was I doing? I'd delayed my escape, voluntarily shirking my seat on the one train out of town, the shuttle to Paradise, in hopes that a girl I'd made a slight connection with would decide she wanted to spend the first few days of her afterlife experience getting to know me. Why would she? What did I even have to offer her? A couple free pints of the worst beer she'd ever taste, or a gratis game or two in a lane where you never could knock down all ten pins. As I walked home that night, I was painfully aware that I'd spent the majority of our single interaction staring at her like a child ogling a movie theater screen. She was a fantasy picture show and nothing more.

That fourth afternoon, the bowling alley was practically a ghost town. I could've sworn I saw a tumbleweed roll down one of the freshly slicked lanes, barely brushing a pin but somehow getting a strike. Jonas and I stood behind the register counter, attempting to pair shoes together.

"Do you know the thing I miss the most? I mean more than anything, the one thing I hope they will have when I am finally able to leave this place?" Jonas pushed his thin-framed spectacles up his crooked nose.

"Being able to actually get a good night's rest?" I scratched at a stray piece of ugly, antiquated wallpaper that had popped up on the shoe rack.

"Well, that would be nice too, yes. But no, more than anything I miss *Gummibärchen*," he said.

"You mean gummy bears? That's what you miss more than anything else?"

"Of course. There is nothing better than a small bag of them. I could even eat them for breakfast." He looked gleeful as he tilted his head skyward, thinking back on his favorite sugary treat, before shoving two mismatched shoes of the same size into an empty slot.

"J, I'm gonna be honest," I smirked. "I like sweets and all but—" I never finished my thought. The front door creaked open, and for the first time I wasn't focused on the agonizing squeal of the hinge.

She swept through the door like an oncoming storm. Hurricane Mia, ready to rip up everything I knew right from the roots. She paused as her boot heels thudded down on the shitty old linoleum tiling. I could see her eyes from behind the counter—pupils widening as she took in this train wreck of a place, blue piercing through the gray. She lit up the Depot like I'd never seen, the whole place practically baptized in that pale blue luminescence, a little oasis in the middle of perdition.

"That must be her, right?" Jonas asked, though he didn't wait for me to answer. He grabbed his half-emptied beer glass from beside the register, an impish grin slipping across his weathered face. Without another word, he hopped up and shuffled into the backroom—a little Bavarian frogman in a button-up and scuffed loafers.

I was more afraid now than when I sat in front of Michael. Then, all I'd had to do was stand up to one of the men overseeing this whole thing, an Archangel, and tell him I was not ready to leave the In-Between yet. Compared to this, that was a walk. I'd stepped to the plate, called my shot, and knocked it out of the park. Now, I had to convince this relative stranger that I was worth getting to know, or I'd delayed a trip to Paradise for no reason other than puppy love. As she strode over to the counter I waved, calling out "Welcome to the Depot!" Was my smile too big? Did I seem welcoming or overzealous? When did I lose the ability to function like a normal human being?

She smiled back politely, which calmed me, but then she made a beeline toward the jukebox. I was off to a great start. I wished Jonas had left his beer. I was going to need a drink or two after my inevitable crash and burn. At least it was only going to be two weeks.

"Teenage Wasteland," she said, resting her hand on the selection panel of the jukebox. The words came out flat and disappointed, lingering in the air like unwanted guests. She spun on her heel to face me as I nervously wiped at smudges on the cracked Formica counter. "You're fucking kidding me, right? You know that's not the name of the song."

I chuckled, but the squint she gave me was not one of understanding. Utter indignation simmered in her cheeks. I was convinced that the ice in her eyes might melt if I didn't speak up, but at the same time I wanted to experience every side of her, anger included.

"Be happy that you can actually put a silver coin in and get that one to play. I know that's not the name, and you know that's not the name, and that's precisely why it's listed that way in the damn thing," I said, still trying to buff out the stubborn smudge. "They do that kind of shit on purpose. Part of the charm I guess. I don't know. I guess Michael probably didn't cover all the quirks yesterday." The smudge grew bigger.

"So, wait. Are you telling me that the people in charge of this place have nothing better to do than misname songs on a busted-up, bowling alley jukebox? I really misjudged this whole afterlife thing." She swatted at the jukebox, knocking it awake. The machine chugged to life with a flicker of neon and speaker static. She was completely unfazed by the synthesizer, still exasperated at the mislabeling as the windmill guitar kicked into full swing.

"Rumor has it, the jukeboxes in Hell only play Barry Manilow. Be grateful this one has a half-decent selection." I was going for disarming. She didn't even crack a smile. "But yeah, that's the thing around here. It's always the small stuff. Your shoes never stay tied, even when you double-knot 'em, and they'll always be scuffed, too. All those glasses," I said, gesturing to the barware behind the café counter, "they're all cracked, chipped, or smudged. I only wipe them down out of habit and because Jonas expects me to."

She sighed as she sauntered over. She placed her elbows on the countertop and rested her head on her palms, letting the reality set in. Her eyes latched on to the five taps on the other counter. Each one of them bore an unimpressive, unappealing, gray plastic handle, grimy from age, with *BEER* written in thick permanent marker. I caught on and shuffled over, grabbing the two cleanest glasses from under the bar and slowly pulling us each a drink from tap number three. I tried to walk coolly back to her, but my foot caught the edge of a chipped tile, turning what little swagger I had in my strut into a shameful stumble. Still, I got back to the counter without spilling a drop, and delivered the glass to her waiting hand. She took a sip before I could warn her.

Her smile twisted into a frown.

"Let me guess, this is as good as it gets?"

"Now you're catching on," I said. "It's so good they don't even name it."

She sighed and took another drink, staring at the jukebox. I turned my back, humming along with The Who, and trying to think of the right thing to say. I needed to charm my way into her good graces. I let her have a moment with her beer while I searched through the shoe racks to match pairs. I wanted to ask her why she was here, but I knew that would be about as graceful as a car crash. I wracked my brain for the right questions, and, spinning around to face her, I was confident I could charm her enough to keep her around until my shift was up.

"So, why'd you get stuck down here?" I could almost hear the iron mangling between us, the first train wreck the depot had seen in years. I'd have had better luck pitching my glass straight at her head. She glanced down into the sorry excuse for a beer, then returned fire with a soul-shrinking stare that should have shattered every bone in my body. I regretted asking her, and I dropped my hand down to the lighter in my pocket, convinced that self-immolation was better than screwing this up.

"I don't really remember," she said. "I died . . . obviously." She took another swallow of number three as my nerves nipped like hounds at my restless, shaking right leg. "I guess I wasn't really the most faithful girl in the world. It's kind of hard to believe in something you can't see when you can basically see anything with the touch of a button. How long have you been here?"

"Twelve years and four days," I mumbled, trying to steer my mind away from the fact that I could've been out of here days before. "Wait, what do you mean about being able to see anything?"

A shifty patron shuffled in from the street and up to the counter. He reeked of bad Scotch, and his booze-bloated, blushing face seemed to be locked in a permanent scowl. His mustache stood out. It was thick and virile and entirely outdated, and I wondered if there was some extra clause in his salvation that said he'd be stuck with that awful black caterpillar attached to his upper lip. I tried not to stare as I rang him up. He was completely dead behind the eyes; they were almost as morbid as the mottled black-and-purple bruise of rope burn peeking out from under his turtleneck. Mia pointed at the burn as he shambled off to lane twelve.

"Right. Wow! Happy twelfth anniversary? Is that appropriate?" She laughed. "Either way, before, on the other side, I guess, you could pull your phone out and see anything. If someone tells you that a giraffe's tongue is black and you don't believe them, all you have to do is pull out your phone and look it up. There's proof for practically everything, except for God. And Heaven. And here."

She looked over at the jukebox, her frown curling back into a smile as Pete Townshend cried out for "teenage wasteland." She mimed along with the band as I pulled a pair of shoes and placed them on the countertop.

"*Sally, take my hand,*" I bellowed along with the lyrics, ignoring my complete lack of talent and inability to sing and extending my arm toward her. "*We'll travel south 'cross land!*"

She laughed as her hand met mine. She lifted a pair of ugly red and green shoes high in the air, and we sang along from opposite sides of the counter. Every cell in my body wanted to leap over the countertop and lift her up, to spin her around and watch her hair swing in the air before we collapsed on the floor in a heap to the frantic violin crescendo. Instead, the song played out with each of us on opposite sides of the counter. Her smile refused to fade, even as her eyes locked on the pink scars climbing the length of my forearms. "Baba O'Riley" boiled to its breaking point and fizzled out, leaving us alone and together, with the slow buzz of the bowling alley surrounding us. She set the shoes on the other side of the register, where they were snagged by a passing lost soul.

"And you? Why are you still here?" She slid her hand up my arm to trace the length of the ragged pink range, raising and dipping slightly with each peak and valley. In my time here, not a single person had ever done something so intimate—caressing my mistakes as if to say, "Yes, I understand, don't worry."

My arms trembled, and she pulled her fingers back as she spoke. "Twelve years seems like a long time. Did you kill anyone?" She laughed coyly. "Well, I guess not, since you're here and not down there."

"I didn't, no. But it doesn't work like that," I said, jerking my arms behind the counter. "Plenty of people around here have killed someone. Soldiers end up here all the time, people who defended themselves, things like that." I rubbed instinctively at my wrists. "And all the suicides."

Her eyes shot to mine as if I'd uttered some horrible epithet or damned every puppy on earth to the supposedly fiery inferno below.

"I always thought suicides were supposed to go to—"

"That's a myth." I turned and searched the racks for shoes I could actually wear.

"But it's in Dante," she said.

"Yeah. And Dante's lingering around here somewhere in one of the slums. Apparently, the man upstairs isn't too kosher with people who know nothing trying to describe the afterlife. Word on the streets is he's not getting out anytime this century either. And I've heard he's kind of a dick." I settled on a faux-leather purple-and-orange pair. They were a size too big. "But yeah, all suicides end up here, because they didn't learn whatever they were supposed to in life."

"Well, it's nice to know that we've at least all got a purpose, right?" She noticed the shoes I'd grabbed and smiled.

"I guess so. I'm not really clear on that one, you know? That's

God stuff," I said. I offered her an equally ugly pair of shoes, a hideous mixture of medicinal pink and aquatic blue. I wasn't hurt when she declined them.

"Does God pay attention to what's going on? Like, does he listen to people?"

"Not really. I've asked Michael. Apparently, God looks in when he's bored, but he doesn't really change anything or make many executive decisions. We're the ones who assume he's up there listening. You can't help but be a little self-absorbed when you're living in a world you can't fully comprehend; and the thought of omnipotent indifference? It kind of trivializes everything, doesn't it?"

"So, God's a grump, Dante's not in Heaven, and suicides don't go to Hell. Am I missing anything?" She mimed writing down each point on an imaginary notepad. I hoped she'd attribute all that information to me, maybe turning the o in my name into a heart.

"If you're taking notes, you'll want to avoid most of the ethnic food here."

"That bad?"

"It actually tastes great. But afterwards? I've never had a quesadilla that was worth convulsions."

Her smile returned, but her gaze was still on my arms. I knew that look. Sometimes we get so curious that discovering some small piece of information becomes integral to our very being. It could be something as simple as someone's favorite color, an embarrassing story that someone won't elaborate on, or a secret letter carried away before prying eyes can get all the details, but until you know, it will haunt you. My scars haunted her, and she was desperate for an exorcism, in the same way that I was trying to fill an entire book in my head with her life and times.

"Did you?"

"Yeah." The word came out terser and more defensive than I'd intended, but I was far from excited about telling that story. The door to the back room flew open in a grand fashion, my ridiculous little German boss stumbling out as my saving grace. He'd probably had his ear cupped to the door, ready to pop in should the conversation get awkward. He strutted past the two of us like he owned the place and made his way right up to the jukebox.

"Just so you know," I warned Mia, sighing as his lanky, wrinkled finger tapped away at buttons. "You're about to hear a whole lot of yacht rock."

"Yacht rock?" She tapped the side of her now-empty glass, cocking her head.

"That's maybe the fastest I've seen somebody tear through one of those," I smiled, grabbing the glass and quickly replacing it with a fresh one.

"Honestly, I never thought I'd be thirsty again, but I just can't seem to get my fill." She barely got the words out before taking a sip from her new drink.

"You get used to that. It never really goes away." I debated whether or not to tell her that she was wasting her time trying to get drunk, but the incessant tapping of Jonas's fingers on the jukebox buttons distracted me. "Anyway. Yacht Rock. It's kind of like that really tacky, late-seventies, singer-songwriter soft-rock crap. You've heard it. Every town seemed to have a radio station devoted to it, with some bad, washed-up DJ. Steely Dan, Kenny Loggins, stuff like that. Anyway, Jonas loves the stuff."

"And I take it that's Jonas?" She pointed at my employer.

"Yes ma'am. Jonas Ehrlichmann," I said, impressively butchering his last name.

"Ur-lik-man!" he hissed over his shoulder.

"Yeah. Jonas has been here for years. And I think this place has twisted him up, because every chance he gets, he puts one of those awful songs on the jukebox. I'm surprised he's gone this long without coming out here and popping a coin in."

"I never put coins in my own jukebox," Jonas chimed in, still focused on the machine. "That would be foolish. Bad for business. There is a code. You press a few buttons and you select your song for free."

"You're going to have to tell me that code, J," I said, tossing a bar towel toward him. When it landed, the towel perfectly covered the small hairless patch on the back of his head. Without looking, he snatched it off and pulled a corner of it through one of his khaki belt loops.

"I will take the code with me when I finally leave this place." He pressed the last button, and a twinkling piano tune cut a swath through the low murmur of bowling alley chatter. I recognized the song instantly and raised my hands to my ears in a futile attempt to block it out.

"Jonas! Are you kidding me? 'I'd Really Love to See You Tonight'?"

He pulled an about-face and raised a wizened finger in my direction, pointing it like a freshly-sharpened saber.

"This is a song that I was never fortunate enough to hear as I danced *mit meiner Frau*. I thought perhaps you and *deine Freundin* would like something sweet to listen to as you flirt while you are supposed to be working. Maybe you could dance. It has been so long since anyone danced here." He seemed to direct his request at Mia, smiling his charming little-old-man's smile and nudging his spectacles. Then he looked at me, the corners of his mouth curving down sharply as my cheeks flushed at his insinuation. "Or you could continue to be a little shit and poke fun at the musical choices of a tired old man."

His eyes welled behind his ancient spectacles and I had to look away. I swiveled my gaze back to her glassy seas, dying for another long swim, or for a simple excuse to get out of showing her that I was nothing but left feet and bad rhythm. It takes a colossal absence of coordination to fuck up a slow dance, but I was certain that, in this love-drunk stupor, what might start as a slow, soft sway would end in sutures and stitches. I could see it: the two of us slowly twisting and turning to this lame tune like something out of a romance movie—a magic moment in time, until the inherent law of the In-Between kicked in and we both tumbled down one of the greased lanes, colliding into pins instead of each other.

"That's really sweet, but it's been such a long day, you know? I can't believe how tired I am." She yawned unconvincingly and stretched. "Do you maybe want to walk me home?"

Jonas had been a soldier back in the living world, and he was certainly playing wingman tonight. Before I could acquiesce, my coat was flying at my face, hurled with exceptional speed and strength for a man who hobbled when he walked. I caught it, though to the outside world it probably looked more like I was awkwardly swatting a fly. I pushed my arms through the sleeves to a soundtrack of lulling piano keys, with Jonas Ehrlichmann humming along to every note.

"Go on, but get here early enough in the morning that you have time to clean up the lanes. Tomorrow is the busy day."

"Jonas, no day is a busy day." I turned to Mia. "C'mon, let's bolt before he starts playing Hall & Oates." Her tiny giggle warmed me better than any coat.

"Wait." Mia stopped in her tracks and turned back to Jonas. "What was the last song you and your wife danced to?"

He wiped his spectacles on the hem of his shirt. As he returned them to his nose, I noted another tear in the corner of his eye.

"It was 'The Way You Look Tonight,' as played by a piano player whose name I never learned, at an anniversary party for my mother and father in the early summer of 1940." He nodded to each of us, then waved us off, turning his back to avoid any further trips down memory lane.

* * *

We hurried into the street like we had some place to be, coming together as the first rush of cold night air hit us like tiny darts of ice. Some ethereal entity had turned the cosmic thermostat down low and broken off the knob long ago. The nights were the worst, when the perpetual winter chill dropped below freezing, and every inhalation was laden with ice crystals vying with the oxygen for precious space in your lungs. The agony was knowing that, here, you'd never freeze to death. Your body would endure every onslaught the wind, rain, and snow could deliver. You'd trip, slip, stumble, fall, and freeze, and though you'd never have to worry about frostbite or pneumonia, you'd still give what little you had for a modicum of heat.

Mia's fingers coiled with mine for warmth. I didn't know if I'd ever felt quite as happy as I did in that moment. Not in the past twelve years, and not for some time before that. We dragged our streetlight-stretched shadows down the sidewalk on Sullivan Street. I could survive even Hell if she was there to hold my hand.

"Where is your apartment?"

"It's above the bakery on Fifth and Vine," she said. "But I don't really want to go back yet."

I held her close to keep out the cold as we walked the scarred pavement. We passed by the train station where Charon sat humming softly and billowing smoke into the starless night sky. Excited faces appeared behind the only clean windows in the city, looking out one last time on the shithole they'd come to know and would never have to walk through again. It was impossible not to feel jealous. I was meant to be on that train earlier in the week.

My mind raced at the possibilities. Surely I was still in the system. We could make a break for it now. We could run through the ticket gates and turnstiles. We could make it. I'd failed before, but back then I was all Clyde and no Bonnie. With Mia in tow, we could bust out.

And if we didn't, my foolish plan would likely add another two years to her sentence, and countless more to mine.

I let the ember of the escape impulse smolder out and sink back into my bones, watching her marvel at the station. I was transfixed by the smoke, spiraling up into the sky in great gray puffs until it became indistinguishable from the clouds. There was no leaving yet, and another group of arrivals would fall with tomorrow's rain. Sometimes the In-Between seemed to kick you right in the teeth.

When she'd had her fill of the escape car, Mia tugged at my hand, pulling me down streets I'd seen a thousand times before. She asked about buildings and businesses, and if there were celebrities here. I did my best to answer her questions. I told her about the restaurants, the brewery, where she could go for a cup of coffee that might pass for decent, how certain saints came down on occasion to check things out. She'd point out passersby: a guy we both thought may have been Jim Morrison, the miserable people who couldn't smile, the suicides, even the sin eater.

"He's a what?"

"A sin eater," I said.

"That guy doesn't look like a heavy metal band." She pointed down a sketchy alley at the old man, who sat not far from us on a decrepit terrace, staring off down the street. A ghoulish figure with an olive complexion and an overgrown beard, he was wrapped in an old bathrobe that hadn't seen soap for a decade or more. The tattered ends of his robe caught in the wind, tangling around the wrought-iron bars around him. If I saw him on a poster for poor hygiene, I wouldn't have been shocked. Though we were louder than most of the late-night foot traffic, his gaze never shifted to us. He continued staring toward the center of the city, picking at a tin of apple sauce, his argent hair tied back in a loose ponytail.

"So, are you trying to tell me apple sauce is a sin? Because if that's the case, I really don't think I'm ever going to understand this place," Mia said.

"I mean, it's not my first choice," I snorted. "But no, it's not a sin, it's a snack. That guy literally eats sins."

"How do you—" She clutched me and shivered.

"It's like a ceremonial thing. It's old Catholicism, I think, something that no one really talks about anymore because it's sketchy. I asked Michael about it once. In a way, it's cheating." I scratched my head, trying to find the words to explain it. "He performs this ritual-thing over you. He eats, he drinks, he says a prayer, and then he takes on all your sins. It's a twisted play on communion, I guess." I shrugged, imagining what it must be like, shouldering the burdens of others in that capacity. "The guy must have a back like Atlas."

"So, it's like a free pass into Heaven?"

"That's what I've gathered. But no one really knows. People tend to stay away from him; sin eater doesn't exactly sound friendly, you know?"

She squeezed my arm, her eyes glued to the terrace as if she expected him to turn his head and spit venom in her direction. I couldn't blame her. He'd stumbled into the Depot exactly twice before, his unkempt mop of silver hair like some crow's nest. He'd reeked of cheap whiskey and, full of fire and vigor, extolled the virtue of his work, aspirating and arguing with random bowlers that this whole afterlife thing was a sham.

Jonas, being the rigid and orderly type, disagreed vehemently, and their debate devolved into angry cursing—a volley of booze-coated arrows, colliding with a flurry of German shells. I cleaned up the shards of at least a dozen shattered glasses after the "debate," and Jonas insisted that I hang a sign informing the general public that those who take on the weight of others' sins were not welcome within, though he was willing to make an exception should the Messiah stroll in for a pint.

"He's pretty much shunned here. You see him around the city, but people are always wary of him. Everyone thinks it's kind of unnatural, and they don't seem to trust him. There's a rumor that there's more than one of him. People swear they talked to him, but they're describing an entirely different person. Some people think he might just be a demon."

"But he couldn't be, right? I mean, he's here, not in Hell."

"Don't know, really. There are angels here all the time. But people say he'll still do it for you if you ask, it's just that no one has the guts to. He's obviously resigned to this place. Everyone else who passes the station can't help but look at it, you know? It's like the hand of God reaches down and turns your neck to face the damn train, to see how close you are to escape and salvation. But every time he walks by, he puts his hood up and walks on. Like he knows he's not getting out."

"That's awful. To be knowingly stuck here forever? I can't even imagine the weight of that."

"This place is probably better than the other option. Besides, I think he's kind of a hero. It's hard to like what you don't really understand, but he seems alright to me."

"That's pretty against the grain," she said. "I can dig that. Besides, it's fascinating." She pulled me forward with her, walking under the terrace where the sin eater sat eating his tin of applesauce, the late-night silence of the city pierced only by the click of our heels and the shrill scrape of his spoon. A gust of wind caught us, and as we shivered together, I caught a long whiff of her hair. The sea salt scent brought with it a long-forgotten feeling of warmth, and visions of beaches and sunshine. It had been so long since I'd seen the ocean.

Other tortured souls would swear up and down that if you made it to the edge of the city, there was a vast expanse of sea, though, like everything else, it was dismal, dull, and colorless—a ghost of the Atlantic. It was hard to believe. Even if you took your day off to climb to the top of the tallest skyscraper, it was all city as far as the eye could see. It seemed like a farce to believe there was an ocean on the other side of the horizon, and who'd want to venture out to see an ocean as dead as the rest of this place?

I didn't count the number of empty intersections we passed through, the steps to her apartment, or the times I looked up expecting to see stars here for the first time. I didn't notice if there was anyone on the sidewalk while we stood on the stoop, how many windows were lit up in her building, or what song was playing on the radio of the car idling at the stoplight. I don't remember if the smell of anything fresh wafted out from the bakery, or if there'd been anyone around to watch us. All that existed were her eyes.

"So," she said, shifting her weight toward the door, "are you busy tomorrow?" Her teeth closed gently around her lower lip, a little half-giggle trailing out to let me know it was my turn to speak.

"No busier than I was today," I said, the words coming out as if I were on autopilot, a giddy grin crawling across my face. "So, if you want to stop by the lanes, I can probably get away with trying to keep you entertained." I sounded charming in my head, but the words came out unpolished and graceless.

Then I was enveloped in a hug that left me absolutely speechless, too dumb to talk, kiss, fuck, or function. For once, the In-Between didn't seem so dismal. Not with her in it. I should've gone in for the kiss, and I knew it, but she was already up the stairs and through the front door.

"Thank you," she said, turning back to me. Even in the dim light, her eyes shone brightly. "This whole transition is fucking weird to say the least. So really, thank you." I smiled and nodded, long after she'd closed the door behind her.

On the walk home I was bulletproof—goddamned intrepid. For the first time since long before my death, my head hit the pillow with a smile stretching cheek to cheek.

6

I hoped my two-week extension would pass by excruciatingly slow, as time always had on early Christmas mornings when I was a child. I'd be up by four and wait what felt like hours to wake up my parents and open presents. That slow march of minutes was all I wanted now, so I could enjoy every one of them spent with Mia. That was wishful thinking, but I remained hopeful, even as the first week blurred by like a bullet train.

After walking her home that first night, I worried she'd make herself scarce, or worse, fall apart. It wasn't uncommon for new people to completely lose it for a while, and not just the non-believers. Finding out there's life after death is the kind of thing that can cause a person to blow a fuse or two. It was a lot to process without any welcome manual or rulebook. Michael said breakdowns happened to the people who wound up in the other two places too, but the epidemic was especially bad here.

There were plenty of suicides who tried again, thinking it was all a bad coma dream. Then there were the good Christian folk who weren't nearly as sanctified as they believed themselves to be; you'd hear them loudly complaining on the corner that they'd seen followers of other religions and even non-believers on the train to Paradise. Some of them just couldn't grasp the concept of penance, or the fact that this place wasn't all that different from where they were before—everything was just a little grayer, and the people in charge had the occasional molting problem.

I couldn't stomach the thought of Mia crying in her apartment. As I went about my work routine, I wondered how she'd gotten here. This whole afterlife wasn't exactly the most above-the-board, well-run organization. Occasionally, we'd get an escapee from Hell wandering the streets, but they'd be snatched up and returned within hours. Mia's paperwork may have gotten fudged along the way, some winged clerk stamping the wrong file or placing her folder in the wrong bin. I hadn't known her long enough to really know her, but she didn't seem like she was incomplete or unworthy of Paradise.

I was surprised to see her back in the Depot the next night. When I walked out of the backroom with a tray of freshly washed, forever-tarnished glasses, there she was in the café. She sat with her elbows on the peeling laminate tabletop, her chin resting on two tiny, pale fists.

"Excuse me, servant boy," she cooed, batting her eyelashes. "Could you please bring me a beer? You might not believe it, but this whole death thing can make a person very thirsty."

"Of course, Miss. You're absolutely right," I laughed. "Whatever this is, it does tend to leave you mighty thirsty. Oh, and I hope you're not looking to get drunk, because that's one of those nice little pleasures in life that we miss out on here." I flattened my hands on her table with a smile. "I'm just going to need to see some identification. Can't go serving minors in this place. Unless it's wine. They're okay with that for some reason, but you have to have a cracker with it."

I gazed into the glassy oases of her irises, desperate to slake my thirst there rather than on whatever we had on tap.

"Ooh, can you cut me a little slack this time?" she said. "I left my ID in another life, and somehow I got here without a passport, so—" Her tiny hand covered the back of mine. Even if we'd both been alive, I'd have gotten her the beer at that point. Feminine wiles were hard to resist, and hers were finely honed with inescapable charm. I didn't time my trip, but I was certain it was the fastest I'd ever returned to a table with a beer. I set it in front of her, presenting it like some great bastion of hope. She sipped on the beer and clearly found it unsatisfying, but that didn't stop her.

"So, Owen. I don't know about you, but my apartment is not exactly what you'd call amazing."

"Is that so?" I responded in mock outrage. I slid into the booth across from her, ignoring my work duties.

"Regrettably, that does seem to be the case," she said. "Not that my place before was great, mind you, but this place is a bit more like a dumpster that somebody's just covered in wallpaper." She sipped on her beer, calm and cool, not even scowling at the abysmal taste, her smile never quite fading as she looked at me.

"That unfortunately sounds about right," I said, wishing for a drink of my own. "Mine's this awful, hospital-white color. It's like being in a psych ward."

"Oh my god, I know. My walls are just awful and off-white, like old sheets that have been washed too many times, with too many dark colors," she said, taking a big gulp. "And the floors are absolutely terrifying. I can't walk barefoot on them, they're like raw wood. I look ridiculous, but I have to wear at least three pairs of socks."

I nodded, remembering the struggle in my own apartment. I could just imagine her sneaking around in bulging, mismatched socks, worried her delicate feet would become harbor to dozens of fresh splinters.

"Trust me, that's for the best. Splinters here are a lot like paper cuts, only twice as annoying and three times as difficult to care for." I felt like a sage, dispensing the great wisdoms of this place while she hung on every word.

"Okay, and hear me out on this one." She lowered her voice and scrunched down close to the tabletop. I followed suit, bringing my face close to hers, our noses nearly touching. "So, the guy that lives next door, left-hand side. I'm pretty sure I know him. I saw him yesterday, going into his apartment as I was leaving, and he kind of looked away. But I remember him from back home. It was a cold and snowy night about two years ago. I was coming home from a bar that I'd snuck into, and his campaign limo stopped next to me. He was a politician." She nibbled on her lower lip, and though I wanted to know everything, I could get lost in that simple gesture for the rest of the evening.

"He picks me up to give me a ride home. After he finds out I'm old enough to vote, that creep tried to peek up my skirt. Can you believe it? I could've been his granddaughter. I was so disgusted."

"Honestly? That's kind of how this place works. He'll probably see you all the time. He's probably going to feel guilty as hell about it, too." She offered me the last sip from her glass and I accepted it, grateful to put my lips where hers had been moments before. "I've got my own thing like that. I had this fitness teacher in high school. I always got in trouble in his class; we just didn't mesh, and I ended up ratting him out for supplying these growth hormones to the football team. It was this huge scandal. He got fired, couldn't get a job as a coach anywhere." I spun the glass on its rim, watching her watch me. "I never heard anything about him after I moved away for college. When I ended up here, I saw him everywhere. I'd see him every morning, jogging alongside my bus, giving me this awful glare through the one eye he's got left."

"Wow. You know, you're pretty open with this stranger. I kind of like that." She put her hand on the glass to stop the spinning, wiping with her napkin at the ring of condensation I'd spread.

"Well, you're surprisingly well-adjusted to this whole being dead thing, and I kind of like you—that. I kind of like that." My eyes widened for a moment, my cheeks flushing a bright red. Her bottom lip again between her teeth, another giggle escaped.

I could have continued our conversation forever, but Jonas looked over every two minutes or so, as if I was supposed to be working or something. Begrudgingly, I gave into his whims, my cheeks still burning from my conversational flub.

She left before my shift ended that night. Rather than slip out silently, she dropped a handful of dull, silver coins into the jukebox and picked "Escape" for each of her three selections. As the opening drum line erupted from the crackling sound system, she began to sashay toward the door, stopping to shoot a sly look over her shoulder as she shifted the door open.

"Stay," I mouthed from behind the counter as I polished a pair shoes. She didn't, but I was certain her lips formed a "next time," in my direction.

Jonas tapped his toes to the song and informed me that I should be so lucky to spend the rest of eternity with a beautiful girl who had such fine taste in music. As he frog-shuffled off to the far lane, I replayed his words in my head. He was right.

* * *

My shift came and went the next night without so much as a hint of her saltwater scent. I considered stopping by her apartment on the way home, but the idea made me uncomfortable. I couldn't justify by saying it was on the way. "Yeah, I was just in the neighborhood, twenty-three blocks across town from anywhere I need to be, and oh hey, where were you tonight?"

That was a foolproof way to shoot myself in the foot. Mia would run away screaming, thinking I was some kind of kook.

Instead, I stumbled home and curled into bed, staring out the window into the starless sky. I wondered if she was doing the same thing on an awful, shabby mattress across town, imagining that guy who served her drinks and offered her free rounds of bowling. I sank a little, the fantastic high of meeting this incredible new person melting away into an uncomfortable, familiar malaise. I didn't like it one bit, but at least sleep found me quickly.

The next day, Mia arrived at the Depot before me, occupying a corner booth in the café with a book in her hands. The cracked, white leather cover looked to be hundreds of years old, though *Bright Lights, Big City* has been scribbled on the front in red permanent marker. She glanced in my direction in a secretive, almost seductive manner, one corner of her mouth turning up in a shy smirk. I pretended not to notice. She returned the favor as I took up my post behind the counter.

"Go over there," Jonas said from some secret place behind me, a little louder than I would have liked. Mia stifled her giggle into a quiet exhalation as she turned the page. I spun around, ready to strangle the life out of the little German.

"Jonas!" I hissed. "Be cool, man!"

"I am cool. The coolest. You have seen me dance," he said, swinging a grimy rag. "But you should go over there. She has been waiting for you. She even asked where you were." He pointed, and I turned just as her eyes darted back down to the ancient book.

"Really?"

"No, she did not ask." He clapped my shoulder in consolation. My plaid shirt grew damp as an acrid secretion of cleaning solution and red jelly left the rag in his hand for a new home on my shoulder. "I was trying to make you confident. Look, she keeps looking at you. That is just as good as asking, *nicht wahr*?"

"Right. That's true. What do I do?" Nerves crawled through

my body like a million angry little fire ants. I rubbed my forearms in a futile attempt to relieve the itch in my veins. If I could just go for a swim, that would cool everything.

"Do you listen to me at all?" he sighed. We'd only spent my past two shifts talking about this. He brought his thumb and middle finger to his temples, rubbing as he muttered something indecipherable in German. "You have not been quiet about her since you came back from St. Peter's. She is beautiful. She makes you do a little dance when you walk, though your dance is not as good as mine. You do not even notice it, do you? You stumble over your own feet like a clumsy little *Hündchen*. Just go. Sit down and talk to her and try not to think so much." He neatly placed his rag in a bucket underneath the counter and picked up a tray of dirty glasses.

"When I was your age, we did not think so much. When I saw *meine Frau* for the first time, I was not much younger than you. I walked up to her and I did not think. I asked her if she would like to walk with me through the park. It is that easy."

The old man clearly had more confidence in my ability than I did.

"Also, I lied again. She did ask." Though I'd heard his life story many times, with his mischievous smile he could've been some little Black Forest imp. As I stepped past him, he offered up encouragement by pushing the tray of glasses into the small of my back, simultaneously pushing a lump up into my throat. The lump perched there as I stumbled like a puppy toward Mia, ready to strike and unload all the words I wanted to say, the feelings I was certain I felt.

It was difficult not to sit across from her in the booth and deliver some long-winded Shakespearean monologue about how she lit up the whole city, how she brought color into the gray, how her glassy blue eyes reminded me of the marbles I'd played with as a child; how I wanted to know every little detail of her life, and why she ended up here, of all places, and if maybe, just maybe, she'd like to spend the rest of eternity getting to know me.

I mustered a nod toward her book and uttered a calm, "So, how is it?" I looked over my shoulder to give Jonas a confident smile, but he'd already disappeared into the kitchen.

"It's not bad," she said without looking up. "A bit more pretentious than I remember, but I think that's part of the charm, honestly. I found it at the library last night. The first few pages are missing, and a couple of the best lines are completely blacked out. Honestly, I'm only half-reading it. I don't know if you know, but there's this handsome man who works here—and the younger guy is pretty cute too."

Her eyes rose to meet mine, a beautiful, cool wave crashing against my body, washing away all the heat and anxiety and nervous second-guessing—a cold drink of water to drown the lump lodged in my throat, toppling it down into my stomach in a torrential downpour of comfort and ease.

"I'm sorry, what?" I surfaced from that cool water.

"What do you miss the most?" she said, setting her book on the table. "Back then? Back home, or whatever. Before you were here. What do you miss the most?" Her narrow fingers tapped out a tune on the back of the book. The beats could have been interpreted as a nervous tic, if not for her aplomb.

"Do I have to pick just one?" I said. I spent the majority of my time here trying not to think about the past, but I fired off an answer from the tip of my tongue. "I miss the musty smell of old book stores. I miss food actually tasting the way it's supposed to. I miss the greasy food-cart grub that tastes like the best thing you've ever eaten at two o'clock in the morning. I miss color—a lot. You sort of don't realize it, but back then, you took for granted how vibrant things could be, even when they were bad. A rainy day here is the same as a sunny day—it's all different shades of gray, but there? You could have blues and greens, whites, even yellow all mixed in with the grays. So, I guess that's what I miss the most. Or sex. Or sandwiches."

"Are you seriously telling me that I can't get a sandwich here?" She raised her fists toward the sky, as if to warn whatever was up there that this atrocity would not fly now that she was here. "Are you really sure this isn't Hell?"

"Of course you can get a sandwich here, but it's not going to be anything like you remember. Unless you ate cardboard sandwiches before." I reached for her outstretched arm and lowered it calmly to the table.

She grinned. "Do people have sex here?"

I nearly gagged. "Well I mean . . . Yeah, I guess they do. I mean, I haven't," I stammered, falling into the rabbit hole of realization that I had never been intimate here, and that I wouldn't know what to do if the situation presented itself. I imagined my teenaged-self fumbling around under blankets, getting absolutely nowhere despite tips that were guaranteed to get the job done. My cheeks heated with embarrassment. "It's just different. Like everything else. It's not that common, I don't think, although Michael tells me it happens all the time up there. I think everyone here is just busy trying to get out, so interpersonal relationships don't often prosper down here. Besides, it's impossible to get off."

"So that's the same, at least. Do you think maybe somehow I was cursed by this place before I even got here, or was I exclusively dating men that were already dead?"

I smacked my forehead, covering my eyes and the dull hint of red bleeding into my pale cheeks. I wasn't sure whether to apologize or not, so I slipped my hand through my hair and scratched the back of my neck as she smirked.

My stomach sank as her eyes lowered to the serrated scar line on my forearm. I dropped my arm to the table.

"Aren't you going to ask me what I miss?"

"Oh, yeah, I just figured, you know, you haven't been here too long," I fumbled. I hadn't even thought to ask her back.

"I actually kind of miss a lot already," she corrected me. "I miss driving. There's something very freeing about being in a car with the windows down, your music blaring loud enough for people to hear it the next county over. And you just don't care. You're happy, you're smiling, the sun is bright, and you're singing along to every word of 'Stay'."

"*You say,*" I mumbled, never one to be proud of my lack of vocal talent. Her smile could've prompted me on stage in front of thousands.

"*I only hear what I want to,*" she finished singing. "Oh my god, I'm going to miss all of my music if that jukebox is any indication." She laughed so deeply that she snorted a little, muttering "teenage fucking wasteland" somewhere in that spirited titter. Her laugh, like her smile, was infectious—the kind you tell all your friends about, ad nauseam, either until they break down and believe it may be at least half as endearing as you swear, or until they tell you to shut the hell up.

"Don't worry, the jukebox isn't as bad as it seems. There are some decent ones in the city too, and occasionally, in the right spots, you can even pick up a radio station or two."

"I also miss the beach," she interrupted. "There's something about the water that's just as freeing, you know? Just out there, floating in this great expanse. You could swim away and never come back if you wanted to. Just sprout fins and swim down below. I used to love to take my dog to the beach. It made him almost as happy as he made me."

Radiant wouldn't have done her justice. It was as if sunlight itself sat in her corner of the booth.

"You had a dog? What kind? What was he like?" I was ravenous, thirsty for more knowledge, anything she had to give. "Did you live near water? Are we talking ocean beach or lake beach? Because there's a huge difference. I always loved the ocean." I was excited, but she seemed to close off a little, looking into the corner for a moment and then down again at her book— the clam was closing around this beautiful pearl. After a moment, her eyes returned to view.

"So, were you jousting?"

"Huh?"

"Your shoulder," she said, pointing at the wet spot, an oozing glob of raspberry jam in the center. "I mean, it's wet and it smells absolutely awful, and that looks a little like blood. Honestly, I've smelled city trash cans more appealing than that. I'm thinking it's a spear wound, and in your spare time you probably do the renaissance fair thing. It's really the only excuse I can think of." She simpered before I could answer, and my return smile elicited laughter that warmed me like a shot of whiskey. "It's cute. Maybe you can defend my honor some time."

"I'd be more than happy to, m'lady." I bowed my head.

We sat in the booth, talking like fools as strangers passed. As much as I needed it to last an eternity, it passed by in what felt like a matter of minutes. Jonas glared at me as he stacked the final chair atop the last table. I couldn't begin to fathom where all the time had gone.

"What are you doing tomorrow?" I asked, the fire ants resuming their slow crawl. I scratched at one of my scars.

"Well, apparently this nice little vacation is over and I get to start working." She swallowed the last of her drink. "So that seems . . . fun, I guess?"

"Where were you assigned?" My scars were very visible with my sleeves half rolled-up, and she kept glancing at them.

"The Office of Records," she said. "Sounds pretty official, right?"

"It is pretty official. They store everything there. I mean, the archives and all. Everybody's story." I moved my glass to my forearm, hoping the condensation would cool the fire emanating from my skin. I feared she might see the scars as a weakness, my inability to handle things. I was terrified she might think less of me for them.

"That's absolutely fascinating! I'll get in good with the boss and see what I can find out. Think about all the dirt you could get! All those mysteries solved! You could find out who killed Kennedy."

"It was the CIA," Jonas said nonchalantly, dragging a musty, soggy mop across the floor next to us. "Everybody here knows that. No one can keep a secret."

Mia pondered this for a moment, looking deflated. I took my chance to strike. "Well, afterward, do you want to get out and do something for a while? I have tomorrow night off."

"You practically had the night off tonight. Schmuck," Jonas muttered.

"And I'd really like to spend it with you." I rolled my sleeves down to cover my past.

She looked up at Jonas, then to me, and scooted out of the booth. The heels of her shoes clicked on the tiles as she walked toward the door. I grabbed the book she'd left on the table and rushed to meet her. Our hands brushed as she took it into her arms.

"I was hoping you'd bring this to me. Since you've given me this lovely gift, I could probably let you show me around a little more." And with that, she walked out the door. No goodnight kiss, no hug, not even a handshake, but I felt like a conquering hero.

Until I turned around. Jonas had crept up behind me. He was disturbingly agile for his age, and he forced the handle of his mop into my open hand.

"Do the dishes before you close. I believe I have earned a nice relaxing walk, since I have done the work of a much younger man all evening," he said, following Mia out the door.

I didn't mind. Something about the Depot at night was calming. The empty lanes, the dim lights, the lack of people. It was almost serene, a feeling hard to come by in this place. I took my time with each dirty plate and greasy glass, doing my best to scrub and clean in a basin that was more akin to a swamp than soapy water. Eventually, I settled for clean-enough and closed up shop for the night. I took the long walk home, thinking about Mia the entire time. I realized how comfortable I felt around her, even with the jitters. How understood I felt.

I tripped and stumbled over every crack in the pavement, jammed my thumb in the door to my apartment, and managed to fall asleep laying long-ways across my bed. I had it bad.

A blast of car horns erupted from the stagnant traffic infiltrated my sleep, waking me like a hard kick in the ear. I swatted at the air, desperate for some way to mute the insufferable noise, but the cosmic snooze button was out of my reach. It crossed my mind that once I left this place, sleep might get a little better. Here, it was the same as it was before I died. Whether ten hours or two, it was a means to pass the time; rest was never part of the equation.

I had been in an abusive relationship with my bed when I was alive. After a long hard day, I'd come to it with open arms, diving headfirst into warmth, comfort, and security. Giving all my trust, I'd fall asleep, yet I'd wake up drained, aching, and unrested. Still, I returned home every night, trusting that it would change. Our relationship was terminal.

After a prolonged but ultimately futile attempt to drown out the noise by burrowing my head under the stiff excuses for pillows, I swung my legs around the side of the brick bed, my eyes adjusting to the silver strands of sunlight peeking through the blinds. My usual morning thoughts involved vulgar tirades against the outside world—casual "fucks" and "shits" tossed at motorists and appointments and anything else standing between me and the repose that eternally eluded me. Occasionally, all I wanted was coffee, but with sleep still in my eyes, I couldn't even get that thought across without a half-dozen curse words. Today, though, there were only six words. They popped into my mind like flashbulbs, one at a time, clear and bright, and without the slightest hint of vulgarity.

I could go for a swim.

Glancing up at the clock on the wall, I was filled with restless ennui. I had three hours to kill before I could steal Mia away for lunch. When I'd left my apartment a week ago, I hadn't planned to ever step foot inside again, except to grab my suitcase. I'd read the three books in my apartment a dozen times at least, and every single one of them had words and pages blacked out, their real truths stripped away and tattooed over with the inky, black "art" of someone else. It was a selfish defacement of art, a flagrant act of delinquency and disregard for an established artistic statement. Apart from that, it pissed me off that I couldn't quite remember Kerouac's line about boys and girls in America. I sank into the couch—not out of comfort, but to evade the incoming cloud of distress that threatened to swallow me the longer I waited.

When I emerged from my cushion cocoon, the twitch in my eye and the quiet unease began to subside. I found my footing on the scuffed and splintered hardwood floors, walking past the suitcase and into the kitchen, where I grabbed the only food available—an unopened bag of pretzel sticks, guaranteed to be stale. I'd had worse breakfasts.

The bag crinkled loudly and opened with a dull, flat pop. I fished out a couple pretzels and tossed them in my mouth. My tongue greedily searched for the sparse salt crystals as my teeth ground the pretzels to paste with dismal, unsatisfying crunches. My swallow was dry, as if something in my genes staunchly opposed this shoddy excuse for snack food. It didn't hit the spot, but then again, nothing ever did. Nevertheless, I reached into the bag again as I made my way back to the couch. Surrounded by the inescapable fog of monotony, I collapsed onto the gaudy floral-print couch that had clearly done residencies in both a nursing home and Hell itself. I devoured the entire bag, aided only by a glass of tepid tap water.

I glanced at the clock again, distracted by the gears grinding loudly inside as if to mock me. The minute hand sat in defiance, a giant middle finger that had only moved forward by a quarter of an hour. I was going to go bat-shit crazy sitting in this apartment, waiting for a reason to leave. It was so easy to fall back into old habits here, even with the guarantee that everything would actually get better. But I didn't need that promise anymore. As I laced up my boots, only one thought ran through my mind. It drove me to comb my hair, straighten my shirt, and walk down a dozen flights of steps into the busy city streets of the In-Between.

I could go for a swim.

* * *

The wind's bitter chill smacked against my cheeks as I marched down the sidewalk, numbing my face but failing to deter me. There would be no more sitting around the apartment, waiting for the next dull shift and counting down the days till the next case meeting, where Michael would request a pack of smokes, bullshit for a few minutes, tell a bad joke, and inevitably tell me that I was on the right path and I'd get out of here as soon as I'd done my time. Through a shop window, I watched morose consumers poking around at used guitars while the washed-up musician behind the counter zoned out, his face painted with complete and utter defeat. There was a lesson in all of this—at least that's what Michael always said; in the end, I wasn't quite sure I believed him. This place was nothing more than depression all over again, this time amped up to eleven, and devoid of therapy, medication, or a working eject button.

A customer shuffled toward a beautiful acoustic guitar, a smile spanning the width of his face as he brushed the smooth cherry finish. He tucked his hair behind his ears and took it from the wall, cradling it close and letting his hands find a familiar place. He strummed twice before attempting to tune, and after a few turns he smiled to himself, satisfied. He strummed twice again, and the contented smile quickly turned into a devilish grin. His fingers began to pick frantically, soft strums transforming into a flurry of cacophonous pangs as the strings quickly lost their tension. His final pluck snapped the bottom string with a discordant twang, cosmic salt being thrown right into the wound. He turned to the man behind the counter, who shook his shaggy hair. Like a child who knows he's in trouble, the customer skulked toward the counter, tugging at what I assumed was the wallet in his back pocket.

I'd seen enough smiles fade in this place, and I wasn't looking to see it again, so I hightailed it away from the window and toward the center of the city.

7

The Office of Records sat behind St. Peter's. Where the courthouse was grand, warm, and inviting, the office building was stark, grim, and imposing. It erupted ten stories into the sky like some modern gothic citadel, black brick and gargoyles greeting anyone who walked by. It didn't necessarily look out of place, there was just something unnatural about it. If you looked long enough, you could see how the angles were maladjusted, the celestial geometry off by just a smidge. It seemed much too small to house the heavenly archives, but who was I to question the logic of this place?

Seven stone steps led up to an ancient oak door. Inside, the sprawling mezzanine seemed about ten times too wide for the building. In its center stood an elaborate fountain that would've put the ones in Rome to shame—an expansive pool of water surrounding an island with a great serpent and an angel. The angel stood tall and proud, wings outstretched in grandiosity.

The typical depiction of billowy, flowing robes and delicate, ornate harps couldn't be further from the truth conveyed by this sculpture. In the angel's right hand, she held a flaming saber; in the left, the severed head of the serpent. The carving was nothing if not imposing. Clad in an impressive set of armor, long hair flowing in an imagined breeze, the angel looked triumphant and fearsome as the fountain water poured from the disconnected body of the beast. Fierce and beautiful, Uriel was cast like an Amazon, a radiant image of divine wrath—the fine art rendition of "Don't fuck with the will of the Lord." It wasn't exactly the friendliest piece of décor to be greeted with, but it got the point across.

I asked Uriel about the statue in my first year. She'd made a habit of coming to the café at the Depot for lunch every so often, always raving about the quality of the food. By that point, I'd eaten Jonas's cooking pretty regularly, and I didn't understand how an Archangel could be convinced that he made "far and away, the best *Jägerschnitzel* on any plane, celestial or not."

Sitting on a crooked bar stool and sipping on a pint of pitch black from tap number five, she was anything but fearsome. Her hair was tied up in a messy bun, and her glasses sat low on the bridge of her nose. Without the wings and the warm smile, she'd have passed for another lost soul in her late twenties. She chattered on about how many hours she put in, how she couldn't wait for baseball season to start again in the land of the living, how she hated the sappy soft-rock tunes that Jonas was enamored with. When I broached the subject of the statue, she sighed. Carving into her cutlet, she replied monotonously without lifting her head.

"Let me guess, your question is something along the lines of, 'Isn't Michael the one who beheaded the serpent with an amazing display of pyrotechnics?' Did I hit the nail on the head?"

I nodded and she looked up, the slightest hint of celestial rage smoldering behind her thick lenses.

"Think about it like this. You've got a book that was written two thousand years ago by a bunch of men. It's not exactly spot-on accurate about everything." She exhaled with exasperation. "I mean, when they refer to me in the scripture, I'm always a male. Do I look like a guy to you?"

I had set her off. She was looking around at the rest of the lost souls, waving her silverware around with purpose.

"The authors put the flaming sword in my hands to guard Paradise, and then they go and shift it over to Michael when it comes time to fight off Lucifer. Now, imagine that for a minute. Michael, who's been smoking tobacco since long before humans knew how. Michael, who can't fly a mile as fast I can run one. Michael! He's the one fighting off Lucifer. It's a total joke. It's a sign of the times, and it's completely inaccurate, but it's not as if we can just jump in and change it either. Barring a full-scale, global press conference, where I walk out in a robe and show off my wingspan to the people of earth, no one's going to put any stock in it. And besides, that would be complete chaos."

Jonas tossed in his two cents as he collected her empty plate. "Michael? In a battle? That guy's a total schmuck."

That was my first real memory of Uriel—cool and collected, but full of fire. As I rode the elevator up to the twelfth floor, I couldn't help but laugh at how right she'd been. I doubted there was a more believable authority figure than her in all of the afterlife, except perhaps the big guy himself.

I also wondered who was responsible for the awful wallpaper pattern inside the elevator, the dingy red-and-gold floral print I'd seen creeping around countless other places. Something about it made me uneasy. I was tired of seeing it everywhere, and since I was almost out of here, it couldn't hurt to take a shot at it now. I searched for an upturned edge with my fingers, imagining that if I peeled it away, I'd have my own little way to rage against the machine.

My dreams were vanquished by the sudden stop of the lift and the elevator door rapidly opening. The wallpaper remained in place, but I'd come out of the battle with a nasty paper cut. This place!

I was disheartened to see someone else sitting behind the desk. I had hoped for beautiful, blonde locks and icy cool eyes. Instead, I was met with a familiar, awful croak, from a frog-like woman bearing an uncanny resemblance to Janice, except for the oversized mole growing fierce and savage on her face, like a second head ready to snap at the thick-framed spectacles resting dangerously nearby. She looked up from her paperwork and scowled in a way I'd become accustomed to. Her nameplate, however, read *Roz*. She must have been related to Janice in some capacity.

"Aw-fice hours ah ovah, you'll have ta come back tomorrow morning." She dropped her head forward, her spectacles sliding down her nose and catching on the edge of her mole. I was convinced the mole had moved on its own, and my spine shivered.

"Oh," I said directly to the mole. "I was just waiting to pick up Mia. We have a—"

"Sit ovah there. Don't play with anything." She pointed with her head, but I could have sworn it was the mole that indicated the couch she expected me to sit on. I fell backwards onto it, sitting obediently until her eyes returned to whatever paperwork she was so rooted in. My hand shot toward the potted plant leaning limply against the side of the couch, and I rubbed the grayed-out leaves between my fingers to calm myself as I stared into the open doorway behind the toad woman's desk, hoping to catch a glimpse of Mia flitting past.

A leaf snapped in my fingers when she appeared in the doorframe with her back to me. Uriel stood in front of her, nearly as regal as her marble statue thirteen floors down. As Uriel collapsed into a chair behind her desk, she slid a manila folder across to Mia.

"Alright, so I've been filing paperwork all day, and that's cool with me. But if he's all knowing, all-seeing, and all-powerful, what's the point of all this?" Mia asked. She brushed a strand of hair behind her ear as she bent to pick up the folder. I stared longer than I should have, convinced I caught her saltwater scent, and the Archangel spotted me. Uriel sighed, sending an impassive look in my direction and polishing her glasses with the corner of her shirt.

"Work. You're here to work yourself out, do some penance, and pass on. Simple enough." She pulled a golden pack of cigarettes from a desk drawer, bringing it to her lips and returning it to the desk one cigarette short. A click of her fingers saw the cherry ignite bright and clear. She was far better at Lucy's trick than Michael. I was jealous that Uriel could see Mia's reaction. I imagined Mia's awestruck smile spreading from cheek to cheek, but her tone remained unfazed.

"Is he here? I mean, is this like the movies? Is he the person I least expect? Please tell me it's not that awful receptionist out there." Mia turned and caught a glimpse of me. My cheeks lit up like lanterns, a stupid nervous grin overtaking my half-interested smirk. I wanted to bury my face into the battered throw pillows beside me as she filed the manila folder away.

"Not quite. First, you're getting your pronouns out of place." Uriel took a few quick puffs on her cigarette, exhaling a series of smoke rings with a smile.

"God's a woman?" Mia called back from the cabinet without even a hint of surprise. "That makes sense I guess."

"Again, not quite. You're tacking gender on where it doesn't matter. There isn't a clear-cut definition in this case. But I like to think she has more maternal qualities. Anyway, you've got the basics—all-seeing, all-powerful, all-knowing." She paused to take a big drag, before continuing a routine that seemed rehearsed. "But at the end of the day, there are over seven billion people in existence, and that's just right now. Can you imagine having a working memory of every individual to ever walk the face of the earth, no matter how long or how brief? That would give me a nervous breakdown, and I'm a fucking Archangel. I sliced the head off the serpent. We're lucky the boss just gets panic attacks." She scratched the tip of her pen in ink trails across a sheet of pale yellow paper, her cigarette pursed between her lips. She'd clearly given the same speech a dozen times before, but this was all new to Mia.

"God gets panic attacks too?" Her voice was soaked in relief. I understood; the thought was more comforting than it should have been, and Uriel flashed an understanding smile in her direction— maybe even through her to me.

"When she gets too deep into all of this office work, she gets overwhelmed, so she's been away for a while." Uriel stood, yellow paperwork in hand. "I like to think it's akin to an extended maternity leave. Let's call it postpartum depression after creating an entire fucking universe."

"Does she do anything?" Mia's question honestly didn't seem that audacious. I'd been wondering the same thing. Uriel erupted in laughter as she shuffled the beautiful girl toward the doorway.

"Believe it or not, she watches a lot of *Buffy* reruns," she said, locking the door behind them.

"God likes *Buffy*?" Mia smiled.

"Everyone likes *Buffy*," Uriel said, dropping a yellow slip on the desk in front of the frumpish secretary. "God's no different from any one of you. Existence is the most difficult thing anyone could possibly do, fumbling around, fucking things up when you think you're doing the right thing. It's why so many of you end up here. But anyway. Rosalyn! See that HR gets that in the morning so we can get Mia a set of keys for the office room. And get a clean-up crew in here first thing in the morning to scrape that atrocity off the wall."

She pointed at the wall behind the desk, where that horrible wallpaper was sprouting from nowhere.

"You didn't have to wait for me," Mia told me over Roz's throaty croak. I forgot the office, the wallpaper, and practically every word in my vocabulary. Her hair was pulled back in a lazy ponytail, but long strands had made their escape, rebelliously framing her face. Her icy blue irises were magnified by the stark white collar of her button-up shirt, and pale legs peeked out from under a dark skirt. I studied those legs for what must have been hours. Though peppered with the remnants of playground scars and what looked to be a cigarette burn, they were flawless. We have to stop meeting like this, I thought.

"No. It's cool," I said to Mia, that foolish grin overtaking my face again. Even in the afterlife I wasn't anything close to cool. I turned to Uriel. "What's the deal with the wallpaper, anyway?"

"You're familiar with Lucifer?" Uriel's voice rose, clear and commanding, interrupting Mia's attempt at an answer.

"I mean, we're not buddies or anything, but I've heard the story once or twice," I said.

"Long story short, after the fall from grace, the battle for Heaven, and me slicing off his stupid head with a flaming sword, the guy got a little depressed." She paused to place another cigarette between her lips, lighting it with her fingertips. "We're not talking a little melancholy. The guy sits in his bathrobe and can't even get off the couch. People think he's responsible for all of these horrible atrocities on Earth, but really, that's all you. He can't work up the ability, or even the confidence, to muster a full-scale assault again, but deep down he's still committed to undermining the celestial authority."

"Good to know," I said. "But what does that have to do with the shitty wallpaper?"

"That's his big battle plan," she deadpanned. "He doesn't have an army of tormented souls, despicable creatures, or demons. He's not toying with the politicians of the world, whispering in the ears of generals, or crashing Buddy Holly's plane. He can't cause a typhoon, a hurricane, a tornado, or even a sneezing fit. He's not trying to enable homosexuality or abortion, and he's absolutely not trying to corrupt humanity through the musical stylings of Ozzy Osbourne and Judas Priest."

She took a quick puff and nodded toward the awful floral-print patch, which had started to branch out. "His big attempt at sticking it to the man is that awful, retro wallpaper. It pops up everywhere here. It's unsightly, and it will give you a wicked paper-cut, but that's about it. It doesn't exist in the living world yet, but we've had it for a couple of centuries now."

"It's in the elevator too," I said.

"SONOFABITCH!" She reached over Roz's desk and grabbed a scraping tool. "I swear in the name of all that is holy, I will take a trip down there this weekend and cut his head off all over again!"

The words trailed off as she stepped into the elevator, her eyes wide with divine rage, her lips pursed cholericly. She must have willed the elevator doors closed behind her, because they came together with a hard clang.

"It sounds like the tackiest attempt at guerrilla warfare the world has ever seen," Mia laughed. "So, do you want to take the stairs?"

I smelled the sea salt as she spoke, hinting at the impending freedom of getting out of the city for a couple of hours, time that would be spent with her alone. The words shot out of my mouth like a flurry of bullets, from the tip of my tongue straight through my teeth.

"Yeah, let's get out of here before Roz thinks we're flies and flicks her tongue in our direction."

Mia pulled me through a side door and down a dozen flights of steps. Though there was no sign of the real Uriel in the lobby, the sword that had been ablaze and in the hand of the statue had disappeared. We shot each other curious looks as we walked past.

* * *

After the long walk to Mia's apartment, I waited on the cracked stone stoop while she changed clothes. I fiddled with the spare change in my pocket, wondering if we'd make it in time, if the bus would show up on schedule, and if she'd even enjoy herself. I was overthinking again, a problem I'd carried over from my life before this place. It was almost unbelievable how in sync we were, and I worried that it was just because she was new—that I was a passing interest at best.

Her footsteps exploded like gunshots as she stepped onto the stoop, mercilessly silencing those thoughts.

"I'm a passing interest."—*BLAM!*

"She's just looking for a friend until she gets used to things."—*BLAM!*

"She'll ditch you in a . . ."—*BLAM!*

Clad in the same ripped jeans and Thin Lizzy T-shirt from the first night, a pair of sunglasses balanced atop her head, Mia also wore that same smile that lit me up and emptied my vocabulary. I dusted off my jeans as she looked off into traffic, her bottom lip clenched softly in her front teeth.

"Well?" She looked up at me. "Where to?"

I wanted to scream back, "The Atlantic! I'll give you the ocean! We'll spend all day in the waves, and we'll avoid everything and everyone else. I've got rope. We can build a raft from driftwood and sail away to somewhere, anywhere better than here." But neither of us would ever see the Atlantic again, so instead I pointed toward the bus stop. "We sit on the green line for about an hour. That's all I can tell you, but I can promise you it's worth it."

She grabbed my hand and pulled me forward as she'd done at the office, cheekily suggesting that "this was not a very impressive attempt at a first date so far." But that slight snark was followed with a giggle, and it filled me with a righteous sense of purpose.

I followed her warmth, contentedly plopping next to her on the bench. The bus would be another half-hour's wait, but I couldn't complain. I wasn't so sure I was In-Between anymore. Maybe Michael had tricked me. This might just be Paradise.

8

The city sat behind us, big and bold against the skyline, brimming with people. The outskirts reeked of desolation and disappointment. The sparse vegetation was as gray as everything else, as if these plants had also done something wrong back in the world of the living.

Putting a used-car dealership out here had been the ultimate joke. Row after row of passable vehicles covered flat asphalt for acres. They inspired hope, freedom, and exploration. If it weren't for the inner workings of this place, it would be hard not to empty your wallet, leap into a convertible, and drive toward the horizon. But there was nothing worth exploring. It just went on forever—bleak and barren landscape, peppered with small groups of exiles and masochists who had shunned moving on. Eventually, the immense and uninviting ocean would appear, stripped of sound, color, and life. The junkyard next to the car dealership served as a reminder that this was never meant to be a place to chase your dreams.

I stood hand-in-hand with Mia as she stared at the scrap heap in awe. Beautiful old cars piled on top of each other, front-ends buried in the sand like ostrich heads. There were thousands. Some looked pristine, but not one of them was ever going to run properly again, though there were always mechanics who were desperate to try. Michael told me it was just another rite of passage; any gear-head stuck In-Between was sure to stumble upon this place eventually and become obsessed.

"Okay," she smiled. "I know things are different here, and I know you've been here for a while, so that's probably screwed up your thinking a little bit, but back in the real world, you try to avoid places that require tetanus shots on the first date."

Towering steel light-poles hummed to life, the manic rush of light bathing her face in cinematic pallor.

"Just trust me, alright?" I said. "This is going to be worth it. Besides, you can't get tetanus here. And what else is there to do in the city? You could go to a bar and drink, but it never tastes any good, and you won't get drunk. You could sit at home and read, but everything's going to have pages missing and words blacked out. I think the movie theater's playing *Ghostbusters* for the seventeenth week in a row."

"Hey! What's wrong with *Ghostbusters*?"

"Nothing, except for the fact that the film reel cuts out during the best part," I said, swinging our joined hands.

"The best part?"

"The scene in the mayor's office. Where Dan Aykroyd calls the guy from *Die Hard* 'dickless' and blames him for shutting off a power grid? The mayor asks if it's true, and then Bill Murray deadpans 'Yes, it's true—"

"'This man has no dick!'" Mia finished.

"Exactly."

"I used to watch it with my dad when I'd stay home on sick days. He loved old movies." Mia smiled, rubbing her thumb against mine.

Ghostbusters didn't seem that old to me, but I guess neither did Nirvana's *Nevermind*, or the show *Friends*. They'd cemented themselves firmly in my teenage years, whereas she was just a kid when they came out—a jarring realization, but it didn't throw me off. That might even be one of the silver linings of this dreary, gray place: kindred spirits could come together regardless of where they had lived, or when.

"I rented it every weekend for like a year when I was a kid," I said, wondering if people still rented video tapes. "Now come on, we're almost there."

I tugged her hand as we wove our way into the dump, through heaps of blown out automobiles—great big Cadillacs covered in rust, busted Mustangs bereft of get-up-and-go, beautiful Corvettes on cinder blocks with shattered windows. We laughed at the men in oil-stained coveralls running around with wrenches, crying out for carburetors and clean spark plugs, desperate to get whatever gem of a car they'd found up and running and out of the graveyard.

"Why are they even trying?" Mia asked as she watched a haggard, bearded man trying and failing to tighten a stripped lug nut on the wheel of an old Monaco.

"They can't help it. Well, I guess they can, but once you're here long enough, all that gray seeps into your soul. You start looking for those little windows of escape. Everyone wants to think they can change things, and make a little paradise out of this place. Michael says you have to get over those impulses before you can move on."

"But don't they learn to give them up?"

"Sure, some of them do. But some of them haven't yet." I pointed at the bearded man on his knees next to the Monaco, twisting fruitlessly at the same lug nut with a rust-stained wrench.

"That one's been here longer than I have. When I came here in my first year, he had his hair cropped close to his shoulders, and he was clean-shaven. Guy looks like he hasn't seen anything sharp since then."

"That's kind of sad, isn't it? It's like a great big mousetrap. If the point of this place is to do your time, learn, and move on, why plant something so cruel out here?"

"I'm not saying it's right. I don't have an answer for it. That's just how they run this place." I shrugged. "You work with Uriel. I'm sure she'll be happy to hear your complaint."

"I guess." Mia sighed and pulled closer to me.

Like a whirlpool in a sea of scrap and junk, the Edsel sat in the center. It was a force to be reckoned with—a preternatural pull, drawing us ever closer. We gazed at the polished chrome, the sky-blue paint job, the plush pristine interior.

"That's what we came for." I turned toward Mia, but she was already running. She vaulted over the driver's side and into the passenger seat with unexpected grace. With a flick of her hair, she nodded toward me, beckoning me to share the bench seat with her, like a scene from the silver screen.

"Give you ten out of my first paycheck if you can make it, too."

"You're on," I said. I was James Dean, running my hand through my hair and flashing her a devilish grin. I took a few steps back so I'd have room, then ran at full speed. I leapt as high as I could and slammed hip-first into the side of the door, landing with my face in her lap. Rebel without a clue.

"I'll be honest," she laughed, "I can't give it a full ten, but you stuck the landing. Silver medal at least." I was certain the entire scrap graveyard heard her laughter, enveloping us all like a blanket. As I sat up, I couldn't help but chuckle with her. I'd never felt this way here. Had I even been capable of this happiness back when I was alive?

"So," I said. I wanted to say "Mia, do you want to just run away?

We could get a car from the lot and drive off. I don't know what's out there and I don't care, because I could spend the rest of eternity figuring out every little thing that makes you smile." I didn't.

"So?"

"So, we've got a little time to kill before the show starts," I said.

"Oooh. A show? Do the mechanics sing and dance? Did you bring me to the junkyard opera? Oh, Owen! Be still my beating heart!" She pressed a slender hand to her forehead in an exaggerated manner, as stray strands of her hair shook her saltwater smell into the breeze. My sideways glance did nothing to deter her as she adopted a barely passable Southern drawl. "Why Mistah Owen, you-ah just such a romantic. How could I evah repay you fo-ah this kahndness?"

I howled with laughter at her hyperbolic display. She lifted her legs up and over the side of the Edsel and planted her head firmly in my lap, looking up into the great big monochrome from behind a scratched pair of aviators.

"But no, really. Are they about to break into a dance battle, because we're going to need some popcorn if that's the case."

In that moment, I knew that this was not lovesick, puppy affliction. The way she spoke. Her sense of humor. Those eyes. The way her head fit perfectly in my lap, like the last missing puzzle piece falling into place. I was absolutely, hopelessly hers. And yet, I miraculously maintained my composure.

"No, not quite. They'll be too busy trying to get these hunks of scrap up and running. Besides, most of them look like they've got two left feet anyway." I glanced down at her. "If beardo over there bends over and starts snapping his fingers *West Side Story*-style, he'll probably pull a muscle in his back."

I reached for the ignition. The keys, attached to a keyring with a dangling pair of dice, waited patiently. Mia slid her sunglasses down her nose, just far enough to uncover those oasis-like pools, and looked toward the key. Her hand over mine, we turned the key together. The ancient engine roared out like a thunderclap, blood pounding through us as our hands separated. The speakers buzzed to life, and Del Shannon's voice drifted out like a soul released. *"I'm a-walkin' in the rain, tears are fallin'—"*

"I wasn't expecting it to turn over," Mia said, wild-eyed.

"Don't get too excited," I said, tucking my thumb through one of her belt loops. "The get-up-and-go is still gone. I tried. You couldn't get this thing out of here with a giant, Wile E. Coyote magnet. She's stuck for good."

"Don't worry, I'm catching on quick. This is the kind of place where you buy new shoes and step in shit right away. I've been waiting for this car to fall apart since I jumped in. You're here to cushion the fall, right?" She adjusted her glasses and opened her mouth to say something else, but the radio howled out and interrupted her.

"Aaaaaaaaaaaaaaaaaaallllllriiiiiiight. That was Del Shannon with 'Runaway,' baby, and before that we had ol' Elton John for ya. Yeah, he shall be 'Levon,' and he shall be a good man, and I shall be the Wolfman!"

The man's voice—a handful of thumbtacks coated in honey—brought an odd sense of serenity. The radio seemed to light up with every word. "That's right, this is Wolfman Jack, broadcasting way out here on the outskirts with a tower full of power. You can hear me here in Heaven, I know you're picking me up down there in Hell, and maybe even In-Between. So, ride with me tonight, baby. We're full of zing here in the station, and it is out of sight. I got all kindsa rock an' roll for ya, put a little pep in ya step, a little life in ya afterlife."

We sat silently as time dragged on, with Wolfman Jack as our wax-spinning spiritual guru. He played rock 'n' roll, and it was alright. With her head on my lap, she clutched my arm with the kind of desperate loneliness that builds up after years of dissatisfaction. The warmth from her body could've lit a fire that would swallow this place whole. To be honest, I'd have been perfectly content to turn to ashes right there next to her. But I wanted to know everything. I fought the urge to ask how she'd gotten here. I couldn't find any scars, any burns, any marks. I wanted so desperately to know, but I settled on lighter fare as the radio played on.

"What did you do back home?" I asked, embarrassed that I couldn't think of a better question.

"Would'a taken you out dancin' but ya too good lookin'" drifted from the static-laden speakers.

"I used to exclusively latch on to cute guys, lure them in with my feminine wiles, and then *BAM*! Axe murder. I don't mean to brag," she deadpanned, "but I'm kind of a famous serial killer. And you, my friend, are lucky that I haven't seen one axe lying around here."

"Well shit," I said. "There's plenty of sharp things around here. I'm pretty sure you could do it anyway."

"Puh-leeze. I'm a lady with standards. It's axe murder or no murder, thank you very much."

My fingers tangled in her pale blonde hair—soft and shimmering, and slightly damp—as I rested my arm comfortably across her stomach. When my gaze caught hers, I couldn't help but blush. I smiled like a ten-year-old on a sugar high. Had she been Medusa, I'd have made the goofiest-looking statue in all of existence.

She brought her hand to my face, scratching comfortingly at the scruff. One tiny little hand sucked the chill right out of the night air. Everything was so warm in that moment, I believed that if I closed my eyes long enough, I'd open them to find that all the colors had returned and the Edsel was up and running; and that we'd never died, and were just parked on some back road in a long-forgotten decade, somehow, some way, still together.

That comforting gesture was meant to distract from the

slender fingers tracing the ridges on one of my forearms, and the sucker punch disguised as a question.

"Owen, how did you get here?"

Fuck!

9

At twenty-one, I felt closer to sixty-one. My life hadn't fallen apart—it was unbuilt, as if some kid had started on a Lego set and given up halfway through, only to come back later and find that the dog had eaten the remaining pieces. I couldn't shake the feeling of being incomplete and empty, a hollow shell of a human being, a cocoon that would one day burst open, releasing not a butterfly but a puff of stale air.

Thinking back on it, August 16 wasn't a particularly bad day, just sort of unremarkable. I'd gotten up early with a full to-do list, yet accomplished absolutely nothing. My ex-girlfriend's bills were still coming to my apartment, I had a few CDs I'd promised to mail to a friend, and I had a job interview scheduled. Not a bit of it mattered. My bed was safe and inviting. It wasn't going to look at me in a worried manner. It wasn't going to ask me difficult questions such as, "Do you want insurance on this package?" or "Where do you see yourself in five years?"

I didn't see myself anywhere in five years. I couldn't even see myself in five months. Thinking five days ahead was enough to give me a crippling anxiety attack. I was fucked up beyond repair, thinking that I was supposed to know the exact trajectory of my life and ignoring the fact that, at twenty-one, I barely qualified for adulthood. Everyone around me was taking gigantic strides forward— framing degrees, marrying each other, popping out babies. At my age, my father already owned his first home. He'd put a ring on my mother's finger and was working his way up the corporate ladder. And me? I was eating cereal for dinner and losing games of solitaire at three in the morning because falling asleep meant waking up to more of the same, tired shit.

I was listless, unhappy, and filled with despair. School couldn't hold my interest, and I dreaded my impending return. I didn't want to go out. I didn't want to stay in. I simultaneously wanted to see all my friends and felt guilty for subjecting them to the gloomy, dismal husk I'd become. It was safer to stay in all the time. I spent the entire summer in my apartment, and I wasn't prepared to leave it come fall semester. I practically made it my own little tomb. If I'd had any business sense I would've waited for October to roll around and charged an entrance fee: "Come one and all, see the hideous ghoul in 221B!"

I stayed in my bedroom until half-past two, only leaving the solace of my blanket fortress to replace the tape in the VCR. Eventually, the sun pierced the veil of blackout curtains, and the glare on the television screen roused enough frustration to get me out from under the covers. I left my bedroom only to collapse on the couch, smacking around for the television remote. The set flickered to life and greeted me with one of those awful afternoon *People's Court* shows. The middle-aged woman judge was squabbling with the defendant from behind an outdated set of bifocals, chiding him for his complete lack of responsibility. The defendant took it in stride, smirking in his pressed shirt and khakis and retorting in a way that only enraged the judge further. She hurled venom with every syllable as she delivered her verdict in favor of the plaintiff, the defendant's smirk disappearing into a scripted scowl. I never bought into the reality of these things. I hated what I saw on my screen with every fiber of my being.

I watched it for another three hours, unable to summon the energy to do anything else.

Ambling into the kitchen after finding a cached reserve of strength, I set about making a package of ramen noodles that had been in the back of my cupboard for at least six months. Halfway through boiling them, I discovered that the package didn't include the usual seasoning. I wasn't surprised. I ate the noodles anyway—tasteless, gummy, and wholly unappealing— straight from the pot, mumbling between half-assed slurps that I probably didn't need all that sodium anyway. The pot and I made strange bedfellows, lying together on the kitchen floor. I lacked motivation to do anything. It all began to sink in. I could either stay like this, hapless and crippled by hopelessness until the end of time, or I could stop it all.

The thought had been creeping around my head for months. At first, it came late at night, like a sinful creature afraid of the sun, whispering into my ear when I just couldn't manage to fall asleep. A part of me was convinced that catharsis would come with the kind of long, final rest that follows a few too many pills, and that part of me grew ever more influential as the days dragged on. Eventually, the thought would come earlier, on lonely evenings when I couldn't muster the strength to get off the couch and go out for a drink.

The thought occupied the couch with me, lingering in the air. It sat heavy on my back, a monkey begging for attention and flinging shit at everything I saw. One day, I missed the bus, and I had to fight the urge to step directly into oncoming traffic in broad daylight. At that point, I knew it was only a matter of time. Laying there, cuddling like a newlywed with an empty pot of instant noodles, I knew the time had come. I peeled myself from the kitchen floor, and for the first time in months, I walked with strength and confidence.

I cleaned my apartment in silence—piling up trash, straightening magazines, scrubbing mold out of glasses that hadn't been touched in weeks. I carried the garbage down three flights of stairs with a smile on my face, waving at passersby on the way down and leaping up the steps on my return. I took a long look around my apartment, properly clean for the first time in months, no longer an embarrassing sty. I would have been filled with a sense of pride and accomplishment, but my work was not yet done.

I grabbed a clean glass from my shelf and a small bottle of over-the-counter aspirin from the cabinet above the sink—the kind of pills that don't do much except thin your blood. I filled the glass with cold tap water, popped open the child-proof cap, and swallowed as many as I could. Scanning my CD shelf, I found what I was looking for and slid it into the stereo, twisting the knob on the speakers, watching the colors on the equalizer rise from a calming blue to a bright red. I melted into myself as *August and Everything After* filled the empty air of the apartment.

I was officially done with this depression. I was the conquering hero, slaying my dragon once and for all. It was time.

I traipsed toward the bathroom, flicking the fluorescent lights on and slamming the door behind me. I stopped in front of the mirror to make sure I could still hear the stereo. I could. The lines developing on my face from the awful combination of too little sleep and too much, they seemed to soften. I smiled again. It was going to be okay.

The shower handle screeched as I turned it, discharging steaming hot streams from the shower head. The torrent hit the linoleum tiles forcefully as I pulled at my clothes, tossing them into the corner basket. The water was warm and inviting and, like a participant in some last-ditch baptism, I almost felt it all slip away. Every bit of stress, every depressing moment and memory, the anxiety that clung to me like playground dirt—I could feel it all carried away by the water, circling the drain and slipping down into the pipes. In that warmth, that relief, I felt justified. Absolved. I was at peace.

I didn't think about my mother, my father, my brother, my ex-girlfriend, my friends, my therapist, anyone. I didn't think about how much every little day-to-day activity hurt. I didn't think about my faith, what my priest might have said. I didn't think about who would have to pay off the rest of my rent for the year, or what would happen to all of my stuff. I didn't think about what was going to happen after. I didn't think to write a note. I didn't even think about how badly the cuts throbbed. I just listened to the music. I didn't pay any attention to how many times I dragged the safety razor across my forearms, or the loud thud as the razor dropped to the shower floor. I didn't notice the slashes beginning to sting under the water and steam. I didn't look down as I slumped against the shower wall. I couldn't look down anymore.

And then I wasn't looking at anything. My eyes closed tight. Even through the water beating down on me, I recognized the tears leaking down the side of my face. I tried to ignore everything else and just listen to the stereo. I sang along when I could, humming when I couldn't. I didn't make it through the album.

10

She sat straight up in the passenger seat, aviators long since removed, staring at me in shock and horror. I knew this without looking. I could feel that tidal wave crashing over me, yet I still couldn't take my eyes off the speedometer, its needle fixed, stone-like, halfway between twenty and thirty. My foot drifted toward the pedal as my trembling hands found their way to the steering wheel.

I hadn't told the story before, not like that. Michael had everything in my file when I got here, and we discussed it, but never in depth. Jonas noticed the jagged ridges and never once asked, but I'd shrug at him during rushes and flippantly mime nicking my wrists. No one on the buses, no one on the streets, no one in the Depot had ever really inquired. Suicides were understood, and the scars and signs were obvious.

My foot dropped on the gas pedal like my shoe was made of lead, forceful enough that I was certain I'd bust through the floorboard. All I wanted to do was run, but the engine didn't roar. The wheels didn't spin. The needle of the speedometer froze lamely in its comfort zone.

"Get up on out yer cars and dance now. Your hearts may not be beatin' anymore, but the heart of Rock 'n' Roll is, baby, and I'll tell you what, here's a little Huey Lewis now, and he gonna give you the news. Yeah that's right baby, he's gonna tell you all about the 'Power of Love.'"

The Wolfman howled one last time, and the radio cut to static before the song could begin. Mia reached across my arms, still stiff, unyielding, and ready to steer this hunk-of junk-Edsel out of here if the engine would just . . .

The cool palm of her hand landed squarely on my burning cheek, wet with tears I hadn't noticed. Instead of recoiling at the volcanic heat of shame, hurt, and anger, she slid across the bench seat toward me. With the guidance of her palm, I turned my head just in time for her lips to press against mine.

Her lips said *I understand*. She didn't need words.

I still hurt. I still hadn't dealt with it. Or thought about it. Reconciled it. I let it happen. No, I caused it to happen, and when I woke up here, I accepted the new order without a second thought. The deed was done, and I was on to a better adventure.

It had been easy to look back on living with nostalgia. Everything here was so gray and mundane, it must have been better back then. And at times, it was—until the end. That last year had been unrelenting and brutal. Every day was a struggle, every mistake seemingly fatal. My only recourse was an equally relentless and brutal act of rebellion. I'd hurt myself physically, the way life had. It seemed like the only solution. The only way to take some control back.

I so desperately wanted that kiss to be baptismal, but it came like heavy rain, knocking me down into her lap, a sobbing, aching mess. I wrapped my arms around her thin frame and held on as tight as I could, the bottom of her T-shirt growing wet and warm. She brushed my hair back calmly, offering whispered shushes and the heat of her body as comfort.

I couldn't find the words to speak for a long time after that, my head resting fully across her lap, my mind and nerves racing, screaming. I could feel it. Every slash of the safety razor, every gouge so calmly scored before, they now rushed the length of my forearms in a frenzy, a full-on blitzkrieg of slices, severed nerves, and shrieking nerve endings. The specter of my suicide circled my forearms, a grim reminder of just how I'd arrived here. The weight of every ounce of hurt that compounded under that heavy mountain of depression was excruciating.

I remembered in full—leaning back against the linoleum tiling, my breathing growing heavy, the water turning sickly pink as the life drained from my body. It had been so fucking slow. Agonizing. I hadn't kept my eyes closed. I watched. I had to. I had to make sure this was it. That it would all be over for good. I sang along through the tears, a mumbled half-singing as I waited for the blood to drain.

I lay in her lap for what I imagine was an uncomfortable amount of time. She seemed to understand, but I was terrified that I'd look up to see those comforting blue eyes frozen over. As I lifted my head, I found the same eyes as before, calming and blue, tinged with sympathy and compassion. I held on to her like the very fabric of reality would tear apart if I let go.

"Let's go home," she said, her hands running the length of my scalp. She slid her fingers through my hair, trying to quell the anxiety ripping and tearing through me.

I nodded, shakily exiting the Edsel. I pushed open the door and held it, half for her and half to hold myself up. She shut it behind us and grabbed my hand, leading me out past the gear-heads and mechanics still fruitlessly trying to restore the classics to working condition. My stare vacant, my smile off on vacation and unlikely to return to this shithole of an existence, I wasn't much for company.

She somehow helped me walk, despite being roughly half of my size. We scrambled over loose parts and scraps of tires, through mud, and across dirt, ash, and the poor excuse for grass that pockmarked this place. What once seemed like an escape was now just another reminder that life was savagely unforgiving. Those feelings always bubbled under the surface like a swamp ghoul, waiting to drag me down into the depths.

I didn't look at the used cars we scrambled past, unconcerned with where they could take me, if they could take me anywhere at all. Maybe I could get a last-minute meeting with Michael and just leave tomorrow. It had to feel better up there. Except for the brief respite Mia offered, this place had been nothing more than another twelve years of inexorable depression, except here misery pervaded the entire landscape rather than just my perception.

I'd dealt with my impulsive nature. Now, I just wanted some kind of peace.

* * *

The silent twenty-minute walk back to the bus stop passed like another twenty-one years of damage, heartache, and disappointment. At least the bus was there waiting for us, and we were able to sit together. She rested her head against my shoulder, and my cheek found solace on her forehead. We napped the entire way back to the city, refusing to take in any of the sights or think up stories for our fellow passengers. This place was cold, and it was empty, but I was blessed enough to have her here.

The green line stopped two blocks from her apartment. By the time we arrived, I'd regained some sense of humanity. She invited me up. I wasn't surprised that her space was similar to mine. I accepted the seat at her crooked kitchen table and tried not to examine too hard.

She put a kettle on and went to her bedroom to change. I waited for the whistle and she returned in a pair of pajama shorts and a baseball jersey. She pulled two mugs from her cupboard, gently placing tea bags in them before the kettle squealed. All I could muster was a quiet "thank you" as she placed the mug in front of me, my face still glazed from the ordeal. I never cared for tea, but I wasn't in the condition to turn down anything given to me, especially sympathy. I clumsily steeped my tea bag, watching the placid amber darken into an unappealing brown. I swallowed every drop, as if this kindness could purify whatever was festering inside me. We didn't speak, but I found serenity in her smile—not quite the beaming one I'd grown accustomed to, but one that was almost medicinal: small but strong, with just enough of a curve to curl up in and pretend, for a little while, that the world wasn't quite so sharp and there were no such things as monsters.

She offered me her bed, but I couldn't bring myself to take it. Instead, I called the couch, knowing full well there was no comfort to be found on it.

"It will be better when you wake up," she promised.

I heard that so many times when I was alive. It had come from my mother, my father, my ex-girlfriend, my best friend. They always tried to assure me, but they were never right. Mia I wanted to believe.

"Thank you," I muttered before she made it to the doorway of her bedroom, "for everything." I expected her to get some rest, but instead she returned, sitting cross-legged next to me on the floor, her hands nestled in my hair and slowly, soothingly working through the follicles.

"Hey," she whispered, her words like a sedative. "We take care of our own, right?" I could sense her lips arch into a slight smile.

I was drifting to sleep when I heard her stand up, her feet

sliding across the hardwood floor, gracefully avoiding squeaks and splinters. She slipped under the ratty blanket she'd laid over me and rested her head on my chest. We said nothing as my fingers glided through her hair, hers slowly tracing along my forearm, memorizing every peak and valley. I let her, my heart beating faster—not out of anxiety, but something else entirely. I was certain she could hear my pulse pounding, and when she lifted her head, I assumed she had tired of it. Instead, she pressed her lips to mine. This time, the motivation was neither sympathy nor apology. Her willowy arms wrapped around my neck, pulling me closer, and my arms enveloped her. As our tongues danced and teased one another, I wanted to melt right into her.

I tugged at her pajama shorts, and she wiggled them down the length of her legs, dangling them from her toes before dropping them silently to the floor. Soon, she was unbuttoning my fly, and yanking my jeans down just enough to find what she needed.

This was something I hadn't felt in so long. The warmth, the connection, the feel of her body pressed to mine—the sensation was unfamiliar and foreign. Now, it felt binding—like a quiet, ethereal understanding. *Yes, you fucked up. Yes, you were damaged, but you are a whole person all the same, and you are deserving of love, too.* It wasn't the groans or moans, the panting, or the sweat that stuck with me. What I kept was that connection. I could have stayed there forever, and maybe, just maybe, nothing would ever hurt again. As she collapsed on me, her bare chest against mine, I could feel her heart beating, slow and steady. It was to that gentle drum beat that I finally drifted off to sleep.

Neither of us came, but neither of us came away the same.

11

Back in the living world, there were few things more unpleasant than waking up alone. I was never one to enjoy the sunlight creeping through the curtains, but tangled up with another human being, legs entwined, warm breath and tousled hair everywhere? That was one of the few things that felt, to me, like home. I hoped, after passing out with her head on my chest, that I would wake up feeling somewhere closer to that home.

Instead, I woke up alone, a spring buried in my lower back. She had scampered off without waking me, but that wasn't surprising. After our rendezvous, I slept like I'd never been afraid of anything. If sex with her was a drug, I'd have been a first-time addict, selling my body in back alleys for just a small hit of that precious serenity.

I reached for the blanket only to notice an unfamiliar weight on my chest. It wasn't heavy, but it was impossible to decipher with sleep still crusting my eyes. I wiped vigorously, and as my hands returned to the mystery object, it became significantly more familiar. A small blue paperback with eyes stared back at me. Not the gorgeous, icy-blue irises I'd grown accustomed to; these eyes were sad and golden, bright lights reflecting in them. An elegant title was scrawled above them, with the author's name at the bottom. As I greedily thumbed through to the first page, a note fell out and landed on my chest. The handwriting was scratchy, but captivating.

> *I found this tucked away in a corner in the records office. It's only missing one page in the middle, a party scene that doesn't have any lines that you're really missing out on. I thought you might like to replace your copy.*
>
> *– M*

I sat astonished, completely charmed at the gesture, and grinning from ear to ear. The barely-blanket somehow provided enough warmth to beat the chill of the apartment. I wondered what Paradise might be like with her in it, and if she'd be willing to share a couch for the rest of eternity. A blanket had never kept me as warm as she had. I was disappointed when I glanced around the apartment to see that she was nowhere in sight.

I looked up at her clock. She must have gone to work, I thought, realizing I was going to be late for my own shift. Jonas would probably understand, so I took my time before I left, enjoying this little place that had become her home. The smell of seawater pervaded the apartment as if it were a mermaid's cove.

I marveled at her treasures as I assembled my clothing and belongings. My wallet and pocket comb had found their way to her night stand, nestled comfortably atop a battered copy of *The Prince of Tides*. I thumbed through it, wondering how she'd been lucky enough to come by a book with nary a blacked-out passage, before setting it down again, knocking stray rings onto the floor in the process. I spent more time collecting the little silver hoops than I did attempting to make myself presentable, but I returned them to their proper resting place, hoping my clumsiness would go unnoticed. I even washed the mugs from the night before, drying them and placing them back in the cabinet.

* * *

Even from her unfamiliar apartment, I knew my way to the Depot. My satellite-guided steps missed every crack and bump in the pavement, and my mind was aflutter at my next move. I had fewer than five full days left, which normally would have been cause for celebration. But the thought of leaving Mia here and having to wait for her warranted a full funeral dirge. It had been just over a week, but I felt like I'd known her for all of existence, as if we'd been two souls encircling one another through the entirety of space and time, from creation to destruction. My hands found the ridges of a few spare coins in my pockets, and I stopped off at the nearest payphone, plopping in the scuffed silver discs and dialing each number with precision and determination.

An awful voice spoke from the other end.

"Hallo! Michael's aw-fice, how can I direct your call?" Janice's sandpaper-throated croak was near the top of the list of In-Between things that I would be grateful to escape.

"Yeah, Janice? This is Owen. I'm Michael's case, and I'd really like to speak to him, please?" She sighed, as if being asked to do her job was an inconvenience.

"Alroight. Yer gonna have to hold," she bellowed. I thought I heard her mumble "ya little asshole." No *please*, no *sorry*, no courtesy whatsoever. So much for angels.

I was immediately frustrated when she hit the transfer button. The hold music was some worthless, nameless, eighties power ballad, the kind I could imagine Michael pumping through the sound system of a convertible as he cruised down some heavenly highway. I could picture it perfectly: his slicked-back hair and Wayfarers as he smoked pack after pack of cigarettes, exhausting every single sensitive song that the Sunset Strip produced over an entire decade. I idly peeled at a patch of wallpaper growing in the corner of the booth.

Click.

"It's the PCH, actually. Err, the Pacific Coast Highway. Sorry kid, I don't think you made it out there while you were alive." Michael's gruff voice kicked in. "We've got a near-perfect replica you can cruise upstairs. And if I catch wind of you knocking power ballads one more time, I'm sending your little punk ass straight downstairs, you got me, O?"

"Yeah, man. Sorry, I was just doing some thinking, that's all." I could tell by his tone that he hadn't smoked today and was in dire need of a nicotine fix.

"I know you were thinking. I swear kid, it's like you forget about this whole higher-being thing. You're right, I haven't had a cigarette in about two days now. I'm trying this gum stuff, but it's not the same. Worst thing your kind ever did, make cigarettes so damn good."

"That's the worst thing we ever did? Not genocide, or war, or that band Jackyl?" I laughed.

"Those boys are goddamn saints, and I'll see to it that, when they go, they get the dignified treatment and respect they deserve around here," he barked. "Now, are you going to ask about a meeting, or are we gonna beat around the bush and get me even more pissed off?"

"I was hoping that maybe we could meet sometime tomorrow, if you had an opening. I need to talk to you about something." I wondered if he already knew what I was thinking and what I wanted to know. If so, he wasn't making it apparent.

"You gonna bring smokes?"

"Yeah, two packs, even."

I picked at the wallpaper in the corner, certain that I could remove this piece all by myself. My pointer finger stung as an awful, thin slice across the tip proved me wrong.

"Be here at one o'clock, don't worry about grabbing a number." The words were clearly spilling out through gritted teeth, and I knew his lack-of-nicotine induced acrimony would not benefit my cause. I had to at least leave him smiling.

"Hey, before you hang up, I heard a pretty great joke the other day I think you'll get a kick out of." If there was one way besides tobacoo to warm the guy's cockles, it was a good dirty joke.

"All right kid, you got two minutes, hit me with your best shot."

"Okay. So, there's three nuns, and they're all standing at the pearly gates, right? They're lined up in a row, right in front of St. Peter, and he's sitting there with his list."

"Mhm."

"So, St. Peter says to the first nun, 'My child, before you enter Heaven, you must cleanse your body of your past sins' and he points over to this fountain." I chuckle preemptively. "The nun looks up at St. Pete and she says, 'St. Peter, I have devoted my life to the Lord.' And St. Peter just kind of looks down his nose at her, right? And he says, a little more sternly this time. 'my child, your body has known the sin of fornication.' The nun doesn't say anything and St. Peter finally glares at her."

"Go on, kid."

"So, the nun penguin-waddles her way over to the fountain, looking a little ashamed, and she washes her hands in the fountain. And then, sure enough, the pearly gates open up and St. Peter gestures her in."

"Keep going."

"Okay, so the second nun walks up to St. Pete and he gives her the same speech, 'My child, before you enter Heaven you must cleanse your body of your past sins,' and he points at the fountain again."

Silence.

"The second nun looks up at St. Pete, and she's about to say that she's an innocent, too, when nun number three pushes number two out of the way so she can dunk her face in the fountain. The third nun comes back up for air and St. Peter says, 'My child, why have you done this?' She looks back at St. Peter as the gates start to open and she says, 'There's no way I'm washing my lips *after* she washes her ass!'"

There was a long silence on the other end of the line, and I started to wonder if maybe I'd missed the click of the receiver. And then it exploded out of him like an avalanche, the laugh-cough combination of a man who'd been smoking for centuries. The coughing fit followed quickly after, and for a minute I wondered to myself if it was possible for an Archangel to cough himself to death. Fortunately, it subsided, and he settled into a comfortable chuckle.

"You know what, kid? I'm actually gonna miss you." The receiver clicked before I could respond. In a strange way, I'd miss him too. He hadn't shared much advice—he basically used me as a cigarette courier, and he was prone to being a bit of an asshole—but he was also one of the few people I had connected with In-Between, and the thought of not having our biweekly visits left me almost wistful. Thinking about it for too long would have me skulking back to the Depot with my head down. I didn't have time for that. I had plans. Big plans.

Big plans that were halted as I barged right into the path of an oncoming jogger. We toppled to the pavement, loud, vulgar utterances escaping us both. The voice was all too familiar. It was the same one that had told me to wear shorts in gym class, and that I couldn't expect to pass if I kept bringing in doctor's notes every day that we weren't playing dodgeball.

We both sat up, and he looked at me with his one good eye and the same scowl he wore whenever I accidentally tagged him with one of those red rubber balls.

"I should have known it would be you, kid." The phrase slipped from his lips like a snarl from an angry dog. I did my best to focus on anything but the gaping hole in his face.

"Woah, Coach West, just calm down, okay?" I said, trying to defuse the situation. "I wasn't trying to run into you. It was my mistake. I wasn't looking. Just on my way to work."

He stood, dusting himself off and adjusting his headband so that it covered most of his wound. I found that more comforting, though I doubt he was concerned about my comfort. Nothing was easy here.

"Right, Owen, just like you weren't looking when you pegged me in the 'nads with that dodgeball, ya little punk!" I had forgotten how curmudgeonly he sounded—like a codger hunched on his stoop, angry at the neighborhood kids for playing too close to his yard. He was only thirty-nine when he died.

"That actually was an accident, you know?" I wasn't even bending the truth that time. Sure, I'd tagged him a couple of times, just for fun, but I at least had the decency to aim for the man's chest. I wasn't an animal.

"You ruined my life, you little shit," he barked, his arms waving unpredictably. I prepared for him start foaming at the mouth at any second.

I hoped he'd extend a hand to help me up, but it became clear that there was no squaring this one away with him, so I lumbered to my feet. I wasn't about to let him ruin my day. I had too many important things to attend to, plans to set in motion. I was Steve-McQueen ready to make my great escape, and I had a girl to bring along with me. I didn't have time for this little rumble he seemed eager to start.

"Look. I'm sorry I ratted you out, but you were doing some shady stuff." I extended my hand, hoping he might take it, shake it, and we could both move on. That's what we were here for, anyway. Instead, his one eye stared daggers through me, and he spat at my feet.

It didn't matter. Today I was impenetrable. I turned my back to him, dusting myself off and running a hand through my hair. I was happy to march away to the tune of his frenzied tirades. I had nothing against the guy any more But I did have big plans.

12

My entrance through the creaky wooden door of the Depot was met with frantic German cursing, coming in loud and clear over the sound of a polyurethane ball clattering down the lanes and crashing into pins. Within seconds, the little German was stomping toward me, his post at the cash register deserted, and one long, wrinkled finger extended toward my face. He cut a swath through a bunch of lost souls wandering toward a café bench. He stopped just short of me and adjusted the spectacles on the bridge of his nose, his eyes nearly doubling in size; a crooked, knowing grin spread from ear to ear.

"Owen, you are glowing," he said, looking me up and down. I wasn't quite sure what he meant. I didn't feel particularly bright or warm, and my clothes were dirty leftovers from the day before.

"Did you stay the night with *deiner Freundin?*"

"What?" I stammered, taken aback. I rubbed at my forehead

in case someone had scribbled "just laid for the first time in twelve years" up there in pen. No ink, just a cold sweat. He wasn't wrong, but I was slightly uncomfortable with just how in tune with me he was.

"*Alte Füchse gehen schwer in die Falle.*"

"Just be cool, old man," I sighed, shuffling past him.

"You don't have to tell me any of the details. That would not be right. But you can at least confirm what I have said!" He didn't follow me into the backroom, so I pinned on my nametag in relative peace. Walking back out, I saw Jonas surveying his grungy bowling alley kingdom, tall and regal like some great Prussian ruler, with his back to the jukebox. And then the fucking piano started. I hung my head, sighing heavily as Bertie Higgins started singing about Humphrey Bogart and Lauren Bacall.

I rolled my eyes at Jonas, but he wasn't at all interested in my cynicism. He walked toward me, singing along with the awful tune.

"*We had it all, just like Bogey and Bacall.* Come on Owen, this is a time to celebrate."

"I am celebrating," I said, grabbing a rag and an aerosol can from under the counter. "See? This is how I celebrate." I started sanitizing the shoes.

"That is not a celebration," he said. "That is work, which you should have been doing nearly two hours ago."

"I was a little caught up," I said. "Her place is a lot farther from here than mine is."

"I knew it!" he laughed. He pumped his wrinkled fist in the air like he'd won a grand prize for guessing at my sex life. "These are not the kinds of things a *junger Mann* can easily hide."

"Okay, okay. I get it, J, you're excited for me. I'm pretty excited too," I said, my back to him as I scanned under the counter for a way to avoid talking about this. I had never been one to kiss and tell, and though Jonas was the closest thing to a father I'd found here, I wasn't keen on divulging all the details to the old man. And if I was being honest with myself, it would have been impossible not to describe every minute detail. Part of me hoped that Paradise would just be that scene on replay for the rest of eternity.

"*Liebst du sie?*"

I pushed spare shoes into properly numbered slots before standing and turning around, a look of confusion and annoyance on my face. "Jonas. Come on man, give me some time to process, yeah?"

"Owen, I only asked if you love her," he said, pushing his spectacles up once more.

I stared through him, listening to the awful jukebox, the bluster of ball and pin collisions, the sizzle-pop of the fryer in the kitchen. What gave me pause wasn't that the question was shocking, or that my answer to it was shocking; it was the sheer realization. After only ten days, I felt a stronger connection to her than anyone in this place, if not anyone before. It floored me. I stood there in a stupor, unsure if my mouth was agape, or if I was drooling on the counter. My heart didn't grow three sizes; my stomach didn't fill with butterflies. All I felt was steely resolve.

"Yeah, J. And I don't want to leave Mia behind."

He walked back behind the counter, placing his hand—thankfully free of the usual damp rag—on my shoulder, and offering a consolatory sigh. Comically magnified by his spectacles, his eyes flickered back and forth across my shirt, and rose to meet mine as he delivered his best attempt at succor.

"I will watch after her. I will even see if I can get Gabriel to take her case instead of that schmuck Michael. We could get her re-assigned here. I will make sure she is treated well. She seems smart. She could probably do your job much better. I do not think she will be here long."

I smiled at the thought, at the kindness the old man had showed me during my stay, and how he was willing to extend it to her. I moved around the counter and toward the café, entering the kitchen without replying. He'd follow. He was sweet-natured, but he was also meddlesome to a fault, as though problem solving were soldered directly into his framework.

"It's okay, Jonas, I have a plan," I said, grabbing a tray of dirty glasses to drop into the sink.

"What plan do you have? You are not talking about staying longer, are you? You do not know how long she could be here. It is your time to go. You have already stayed longer than you should have." He spoke with genuine paternal concern.

"You're one to talk, old timer. But no, no, it's not like that. We're both going to get out of here."

"*Ach, Mensch!* Please do not break the laws. You will get the both of you stuck here for even longer!"

"J, I'm not breaking a single law. I'm following them all to the letter. I'm just, you know, going to use a loophole."

"A loophole? There are no loopholes here. You do your penance, and then you leave. Unless a schmuck like Michael lets you stay longer than you should."

"That's where you're wrong, Jonas. You're forgetting something. The sin eater."

His eyes widened in rage and the lines in his face deepened. "*Ach du Scheiße!* That is not even remotely an option. That is cheating. Nobody will learn anything. You will take that girl's lesson from her. Owen, that is not something you have any right to do."

I'd pegged the old man as a hopeless romantic type. He talked about his wife the way few men ever do, so his reaction surprised me. I hadn't expected a lavish parade or confetti and streamers, but a little frog-like high-five for beating the system would have been encouraging. It was the only time he'd truly lost his temper with me, and I could feel myself shrinking.

"This is not the right way to do things. This is selfish of you." He pushed me out of the kitchen, a tray of mostly-clean glasses in my hands clattering against my chest as my lower back hit the café countertop. My head tilted back just far enough to see an Archangel standing above me, glowering down.

"I was wondering when we were going to get some service." Uriel stood in the café, wings tightly reigned in. Her hair hung loose in a half bun and her glasses were slightly smudged. Her look of annoyance slowly faded, but something else caught my eye. A glowing beacon demanding the attention of all available senses, Mia emerged from behind Uriel. The smell of salt, those icy blue eyes, a coy smile, and a wave were all it took to turn me into a scatterbrained schoolboy.

Like a punch-drunk fool, I dropped the tray. The glasses shattered at my feet, and all I could do was smile.

I was completely fucked, bending over and banging my head into the counter, collecting tiny little nicks all over my hands in my mad rush to clean the mess up. I dropped shards and slivers onto the tray.

"Just a sec, guys, and I'll grab you something," I called up to the counter, thankful that I could hide my embarrassment for a moment.

"Jonas can help us," Uriel said.

I was grateful, my cheeks still flushed from Mia's little wave and smile. It was impossible not to think back on the night before, and my memories had turned me into a total buffoon. I kept hidden. Down on my knees, I pulled a small brush and dustpan from the ledge to sweep up the last of the little gray slivers. A few clung to the cracks in the tiles, no matter the angle or force with which I wielded the brush. I stayed down there, pretending what I was doing was useful, until a natural tint had returned to my cheeks.

"I would be happy to help," Jonas said, shuffling past me. "*Was kann ich Ihnen bringen?*"

"Jonas, you're still as sharp as a tack. You know exactly what I want," Uriel cooed. It wasn't quite flirtatious, but it was honey-coated, the way any beautiful woman might talk to a charming elder.

"Ah yes, but not her," Jonas said, smiling at Mia. She looked at me for help, her face perplexed, but when I caught sight of her eyes, I reverted to that dumb, thirsty ape, dying for another swim.

"I'm not quite sure," she said. "I've never had German before."

"Just get her the same, Jonas," Uriel laughed.

I sliced my hand across my neck to indicate what a poor decision that was, but Jonas had already hopped off to the kitchen. I shrugged an apology to Mia and noticed Uriel staring at me, the way a parent does when they're trying to determine the authenticity of an excuse they've just been given. I turned to empty the broken glass into the trash.

"Owen!" Uriel called. "Be a dear, get us each a drink?"

I cringed at the knowing tone of her voice. If she knew what I was thinking, I was certain Michael must have too. I began mentally preparing for a severe tongue-lashing. I could already feel the fires of eternal damnation lapping at the soles of my worn-out shoes. I grabbed two empty glasses from behind the counter and placed them under taps three and five. I tried to look cool as I did it, like someone in a movie, but I wasn't particularly successful. The beers at least came out alright, with not much of a foam head.

"So, Owen. You're still here, huh? How'd that happen?" Uriel's perfectly manicured nails tapped the side of her glass.

"Uh . . . Michael decided that I still had a few things to learn before I was ready to go."

"You were supposed to leave?" Mia looked up from her beer.

"Believe it or not, he was due out the same day you came in," Uriel said. "Funny how things work out, huh?" Her mischievous banter made me supremely uncomfortable. The pink mountain ranges on my forearms started to tremble, and an avalanche of nerves spread up my arms and down into my body, filling every vein with tremors of anxiety and rattling the blood close enough to my skin for a full body flush. I was a bright red beacon, a fucking clown nose with a name-tag, staring at Uriel, almost literally caught red-handed.

"Well, I mean . . ." I couldn't reveal to Mia that I'd stayed here exclusively to get to know her. I wracked my brain for something that could save me from that pathetic truth. "Honestly, he was right, though. I hadn't really come to terms with how I landed here until last night. It was really, uh . . ."

"Emotional," Mia interjected, the super-heroine I desperately needed.

"Yeah," I said, my skin cooling. "Yeah, it was really heavy and powerful. I think that when we meet again, Michael will see that." I grabbed a rag from the counter and wiped at the taps to avoid where the conversation might be going, but Uriel was enjoying herself too much.

"And that's in just a few days, isn't it?" Uriel smirked. "You've got, what, about four days left?"

"You're leaving in four days?" Mia's voice was calm, but her eyes told a different story. A confounding rush of emotions dueled it out in my stomach: elation over the clear fact that she didn't want me leave, and intense disappointment with myself for putting her in emotional duress.

Brandishing two lovingly-prepared plates of *Jägerschnitzel*, Jonas burst through the kitchen door just in time to put an end to Uriel's inquisition. For possibly the only time in recorded history, I was saved by breaded pork cutlets.

"Now this is a treat, *fräulein*. You will be very pleased. This was the favorite dish of *meine Frau,* and she had a very refined palate." He was practically beaming as he propped his elbows on the counter to watch his customers dig into their food.

"It's absolutely wonderful," Uriel exclaimed between bites. "When you finally leave I'll be so disappointed. I'll have to find good German food all over again."

"Ah, but you have all of the records at your disposal, so you can do that easily. I cannot be the only old man in this city who knows how to cook," Jonas laughed heartily.

"You know, Jonas, you've been here a long time," Uriel said. "I can talk to Gabriel. I think you've more than done your time here."

"Ah yes. Well, that is very kind of you. But I am not so sure. I still have things I am atoning for."

"What kinds of things?" Mia asked, her eyes brimming with curiosity as she tore at her *schnitzel*.

"Oh no, that's not the kind of story that needs to be told right now," Uriel said.

The old man wasn't embarrassed, but he was reserved with his past, like most of us in the In-Between. Thinking about it tended to bring back a flood of memories you hadn't quite dealt with. As I'd learned the night before, it could rattle you to your very core. When Jonas first told me his story, twelve years ago, he'd become a sobbing mess—and that had been after twenty-three years of penance.

"Uriel," he said. "I do not mind. If *das Mädchen* wants to hear my story, I can tell it to her." I pulled two more glasses from behind the counter, filling and placing them both at his side. I poured one for myself as well. Even knowing what was coming, I was not prepared to hear it again.

13

"*J*adem *das Seine*. To each what he deserves."

Jonas could never forget those words, even if they were scrubbed from his eyes, brain, and heart. He saw them every day, in great iron lettering above every building he entered. There was no escape.

"I was born in Leipzig just after the end of *des Großen Krieges*. My father returned from the Great War and took a job at *Leipziger Baumwoll Spinnerei*, the local cotton mill. My mother was so happy that he had come home in one piece." It was that very night that Jonas was conceived. "They were absolutely wonderful parents; I do not believe I could have been more loved."

Though his country was slow to recover from the first World War, the cotton mill afforded his father enough to care for the family; his mother only occasionally had to clean the homes of the wealthy. His father promised to provide them both with the life he never had as a child, as all fathers do, and it was rare that he would collect a paycheck without stopping at the shops on the way home.

"I grew to love the end of the week, when my father would arrive home with his pay packet, and just for me, a big bag of *Gummibärchen*. I would devour them before anyone could stop me. My mother warned me that I would never grow up to be strong, that I would spoil my dinner and lose my teeth." His father would laugh, saying it was better that he experienced the little gelatin bears than the big hairy things that the Russians worshipped. His mother would sigh, serving up a dinner young Jonas would barely touch.

"I grew up strong, though, just as they both wanted. I received top marks in my schooling, and my physical fitness was among the best of any boy in the city." It was often suggested that he should join the growing military, which had been limited after the war, but Jonas never thought himself a soldier. "I loved Leipzig. I could not imagine a need to ever leave, especially for something as horrendous as war. I saw the veterans who had not been quite so lucky as my father. Men with missing limbs, with grotesque faces, men who blamed all their troubles on those who were different from them. It was not the life for me."

Even if the regimented life of the military had appealed to him, he had already met Anneliese. "She lived two streets over, with *ein Soldat* for a father. The war left him confined to a wheelchair, with no way to support the family. Her mother did things she was not proud of to keep food on the table. We played together as children; I would share my *Gummibärchen* when I could sneak them from the house."

Even that young, he knew she was something special. She became the very embodiment of perfection in his eyes. She was intelligent, caring, and beautiful too. As they grew into adolescence, he often found her in the city's center, sitting under a tree with a book. He was swept away as her eyes greedily consumed every word from the page. Jonas would stop by and sit, sharing an apple, or a sandwich, or even *Gummibärchen* he'd purchased with the *geld* from delivering the newspapers early in the morning. She always gratefully accepted, smiling at him in a way that could have melted the harshest of winter snows. He truly believed that no other creature on the planet was created in the same way as Anneliese.

"One summer's day, not long before the world changed for the worse, I asked her to take a walk with me." They strolled around the city center, walking under the trees, across the mostly empty streets, and eventually into the forest. "We decided to play a game of hide-and-go-seek. It may have been her idea; some of the memories have gotten hazy. I found her very easily, hiding in a knotted stump, the white linen of her skirt speckled brown at the hem. She told me to go hide as she stole a few stray gummies from my breast pocket."

Jonas did as he was told, running as quietly as he could through the woods. He found the thickest, widest tree and pressed his back to it, quieting his breath to a level not even a dog could detect. Jonas closed his eyes and prepared as her voice filtered between the trees, calling out for him.

"She would call my name, laughing, but I would not answer. I stood rigid, like a great statue, my body pulled together in a tight ball, breathing as quietly as possible. I would not be found."

And then Jonas felt something delicate and warm that he had never before experienced—the soft velvet of her lips upon his, the rush of blood throughout his entire body. He opened his eyes to what Jonas described as the most beautiful creature in all of creation gifting him with an incredible honor. "I kissed her back, as best as I knew how. It could not have been awful, as she wrapped her arms around me. It was only for minutes, but they are minutes I will never forget for the rest of eternity."

Six months later, Jonas and Anneliese were married. Jonas said it was blissful. Like his father, Jonas worked at *die Spinnerei*, putting in long hours, toiling hard enough that his bride wouldn't have to work. He promised to keep her safe and happy, to give her a home, and to provide support, no matter the cost.

Two years later, Jonas was conscripted. At the train station, he promised Anneliese he'd return to her as soon as he could, and that he would return the same man she had married.

"I was able to keep only one of those promises. My early hunting trips with my father and my ability with a rifle made me useful, but I was not put on the front lines. I was told by an officer that I would serve a greater purpose. That I would be a guard of utmost importance. In the fall of 1940, I was put on a train to Weimar, to serve as a tower guard for a work camp that had been opened, a place called *Buchenwald.* My stomach sank at those iron gates. *Jadem das Seine* hung like the heaviest of sentiments upon my heart." He sighed, looking down into his glass as his past trickled from his tongue. Uriel slowly closed her eyes, clenching them hard for a moment, knowing how his story played out. Jonas placed his emptied glass under the tap and refilled as he continued. "*Meine Vorgesetzen* were terse and direct with their orders. I was not to interact with the prisoners in any way."

Jonas was told that these people were criminals or enemies of the *Reich*. He would sit in a guard tower for endlessly long shifts, watching like a hawk over the gates surrounding the camp and the beech trees in the distance. He was provided good meal and drink, warmth, and—most importantly—a rifle.

"Under no circumstances could I allow any prisoner to escape. Any one of them could be dangerous: a conspirator with the Allies, a courier of political secrets, a revolutionary seeking to undermine and destroy our homeland. But as I looked out at them, that was not what I saw. I saw frail, weak men who could not have run anywhere, women and children who surely had no wishes other than to return to their own homes, to play games as I had as a child. But I had no choice."

Jonas heard that the last tower guard who refused to obey an order was treated as a turncoat and thrown in among the prisoners, clad in the same drab rags, eating slop and making bullets in a factory as if he were a slave. Bullets that Jonas would be expected to use if the turncoat ever tried to escape. With great reluctance and a leaden weight on his heart, Jonas agreed to be a tower guard. "I was at least able to find comfort in my *Mitkämpfer*, who in secret would admit their reluctance for the barbaric methods our *Kommandanten* insisted upon."

On a snowy November evening, Jonas received a letter from Anneliese. The summer would bring them a baby, and though he wouldn't be there for the birth, Anneliese promised she would tell their child how great papa was, how he was defending the fatherland, and how he would return to them soon, strong and proud, as a hero.

"At the time, I truly believed that winter would be the hardest for me. Away from my pregnant wife, stationed in a little outpost, the rifle became an extension of my hands." He found no joy in shooting an escaping prisoner, no satisfaction in having done his duty. It was an order followed only so that he could return to his family, to see his wonderful wife and the new life they would welcome with open arms. Every pull of the trigger became a colossal endeavor, as if the weight of the entire world acted as the resistance. Every bullet was accompanied by a silent prayer. He never found the courage to watch the white snow turn deep red as the explosion echoed through the forest.

"It happened too many times that first winter." His breathing grew heavier as his story continued, fogging his spectacles with a small layer of moisture. He gently tugged them off to clean them, revealing the growing redness in his eyes, tear ducts ready to burst at any moment. The Depot was quiet, every heart sinking as all ears tuned into the old man's tale.

The spring brought him little in the way of respite. From his guard tower, Jonas saw brutality that deeply saddened him, acts he believed he himself would never be capable of. Men who had confessed to him the inherent evil of the camp seemed to eagerly participate in the kind of savagery Jonas had long thought impossible in civilized men. Children were brutally beaten, prisoners raped, mothers starved. Jonas saw the men's shimmering, gleeful eyes as they tightened the nooses, their sickening smiles as they placed the tips of their guns against frail young heads.

"I believed I could no longer bear it. Surely if there was a God, he would not condone such atrocities."

Then summer came, and with it a new letter from Anneliese. Their daughter had been born on the sixteenth of June, 1941. Monika Ehrlichmann was a healthy, beautiful baby girl, with small wisps of blonde hair. Anneliese said that she had Jonas's smile, and her eyes.

"I was so overcome with joy at my little *Mäuschen* that for a time I became numb to the things I was tasked to do. It never truly became easier."

As summer faded into autumn, Jonas focused only on the prisoners trying to escape, and desperately hoped for word from his family. Every new letter gave him renewed purpose. Anneliese longed for him and promised a hero's welcome when he returned. She said their daughter would be proud of his service.

"I did not have the heart to tell her that even I was not proud of what I had done. I would not be deserving of even a criminal's welcome. Every season, I would receive a new letter, sometimes two. Monika had been given a beautiful dress from my parents. And though she was much too young for serious lessons, Anneliese wrote that our little *Mäuschen* would tap on the piano keys and sing along in her own little way."

Those little things kept Jonas grounded. He was more than a soldier, more than a watchtower guard and reluctant executioner. He was a beaming father, graced with a daughter already interested in the arts, in giving something back to the world despite its cruelty.

The letter that came in the winter of 1942 was perhaps the most difficult one Anneliese ever wrote––it was certainly the hardest thing Jonas would ever read. Her mother had been taken by the SS. She was half-Romani, nothing more than a "gypsy whore," who was poison to the *Reich*. Anneliese was heartbroken. Even worse, it happened in front of Monika, who was far too young to understand why these men were forcefully taking her grandmother away.

"I did not have the heart to write back and tell her that I already knew. She had been put on a train, and that train dropped her in front of those awful, iron letters."

Jadem das Seine.

Anneliese's mother had always been a fighter, supporting her family when her husband came back maimed. She was a strong woman, and Jonas had seen that same spirit manifest in Anneliese. But *Buchenwald* was practically a death sentence. Jonas saw his mother-in-law routinely beaten by his fellow *Wachen*, men whom he had considered friends. She had been denied meals and forced to work harder hours than others, leaving her hands crippled by the factory work—and she was taken to officers' quarters to be passed around like a child's toy. Jonas could do nothing to save her.

"I had let down my wife and daughter. My heart was torn asunder. That pain was truly *der Weltschmerz*, the ultimate betrayal to my family."

In the early winter of 1943, *der Kommandant* stood guard with Jonas. Jonas was commended on his excellent work, his perfect marksmanship, and the great service done for the *Reich*. No matter what anyone had to say to the contrary, they were winning the war and doing the right things in the process.

"I looked at the wooden butt of my gun—so many scratch marks, each to memorialize a life I had taken, a life I had prayed for as I did my duty. I never had to shoot more than once, but I made that one shot more times than I could count. Many more times than I will ever forget. As we stood by lantern light, staring out into the falling snow, we both caught sight of something creeping past the gates. The brown rags were unmistakable. Numb, I lifted my rifle, ready to show my superior that his faith in me had not been misplaced. And then she looked up. Even without the light of the lantern, I would have recognized that face. It was Anneliese's mother."

Tired of the beatings, the labor, the rape, she had decided to brave an escape through the forest in the dead of winter rather than suffer one more day of torment. Jonas could not blame her. In truth, he wanted to be with her, to guide her past the large rocks and broken branches, to provide his coat for her warmth. He was certain he could guide her all the way back to Leipzig, 100 kilometers northeast through the winter snow, emboldened by the desire to see his family.

"If we could have marched through the night, we would have been home the very next day. But it was something I could not do."

He raised his rifle, jamming the scarred butt hard into his shoulder. His eyes welled with tears as his finger moved slowly toward the trigger. The burning stare of his commanding officer darted between Jonas and the escapee.

"I knew that if I did not shoot, my rifle and coat would be taken. I would be thrown down among the rest of those that we held for being different. I would become *der fiend*. And that would be if I was lucky. More likely, I would be marched to the gallows, or immediately executed with the *Mauser* pistol tucked underneath the officer's woolen overcoat. In this moment I knew there was no salvation, and yet I silently prayed for hers."

Jonas paused his tale and inhaled deeply, holding his breath before slowly allowing it to vibrate from his lungs. I kept my eyes to the ground, unable to bear the heartache on his face.

The sound of the gun ricocheted through the cold winter wind, echoing between the branches of the beech trees he had watched over for years. A brand new swath of red stained the freshly fallen snow.

"I asked *meinen Hauptmann* if I could be removed from my post for the night." Jonas convinced the commanding officer he was coming down with some sort of illness and spent the rest of the night slumped over in the latrine, emptying his stomach and his guilt. "I was admitted to our hospital ward with fever and kept for nearly a week. All I had wanted was pen and paper to write to my wife. To apologize for what I had done. But even if they had obliged, I had no idea what to tell her. I could not bring myself to write it out. Even in the simplest of terms. I am sorry, Anneliese. Your mother was placed here in Buchenwald, and I had no choice but to take her life."

He struggled with it for two full seasons, still stuck high upon the wall in his guard post, still saying a prayer for every unfortunate life he had to take. It had almost gotten easier for him. He knew that no matter what, he could do no more damage to his family; only he would have to shoulder this burden.

He was not prepared for the letter that came the next autumn.

The Allies had bombed Germany. Leipzig wasn't entirely destroyed, but the city center was forever changed. The church where Jonas and Anneliese had married was reduced to rubble, and the gardens they walked through as sweethearts had been scorched. The great fire that fell from the sky had been difficult to contain, and there were far too many unnecessary deaths. The letter did not come from Anneliese, his parents, or even her father. It had been issued by the *Reich*.

"I would never get the chance to explain myself. To apologize. To see my beautiful daughter."

Jadem das Seine.

14

Jonas finished his story and, in the resulting silence, another pint. Looking past his audience, he wiped his sleeve against his mouth. A long, deep inhale accompanied the removal of his spectacles. He wiped at them fiercely with the bottom hem of his shirt, erasing away the smudges and tear stains before shuffling into the backroom.

I leaned back against the wall, crossing my arms as Uriel looked down somberly at her empty plate. Mia's eyes radiated heartbreak, and her mouth hung slightly agape.

"He's been absolved since long before Owen got here," Uriel muttered, not yet looking up from the emptied dish. "At least as far as we're concerned. He won't let go, though. He's stubborn, holding onto those past sins. It frustrates Gabriel to no end."

I nodded, looking at their sullen faces. As many times I'd heard the story, especially on long nights when he'd had too much to drink in a failed attempt at inebriation, and played the saddest songs on the jukebox, it split me in two as easily as the first time.

"After the war, he worked in a bicycle factory," I added, trying to cheer them up. "He made children's bicycles after he was discharged, right up until the day he died. I think he saw it as a small atonement."

My words didn't help much. I collected their plates and scuttled off to the kitchen. Jonas was huddled over the sink, vigorously scrubbing what may have been the cleanest plate in the whole place, as though if he could return it to an impossibly pristine white, it would take away his frustration and guilt. I set the plates on the countertop and squeezed his shoulders, the same way my father did when I was young.

"Please, Owen," he said. "Not right now. Go and attend to the customers."

I wished I could do something that would get him back to his usual jovial, hoppy self. I grabbed a cleaning rag and headed to the jukebox. I hoped "Escape" would do the trick, but even as the song drifted through the nearly empty alleys and lanes, I didn't hear a single loafer-toe tap. I left him to his dishes and returned to the lunch counter as he had asked. Uriel had already disappeared, leaving payment for their meals and a generous tip.

Mia looked up, her head in her hands. I transferred the money into the beat-up old cash register, waiting for the other shoe to drop.

"You're leaving soon?" She had a knack for asking a question that pierced straight to the heart of the matter, as if she'd learned linguistics from an archer.

"I was supposed to be, yes," I said, avoiding her eyes for what must have been the first time. "But Michael said that I wasn't quite ready yet. Remember?"

"Right, but that was before," she said. "We're talking about now. You could be gone by the end of the week?"

"I. Look. I don't know. I don't know what Michael's going to say. You met him; he's more mob boss than Archangel. I can't predict him. But what about this. What if I can get both of us out at the same time?"

She looked at me warily, puzzled. "But we've been spending all this time together." The words came out in a huff, and I wondered if the blue in her eyes would start to boil. "How could you just not tell me that you could be leaving at any fucking minute?" Her hands clenched around her empty pint glass, one pointer finger picking at the chipped red nail polish on the opposite hand.

"Look, I can't explain just yet, but I've been thinking about something. A plan. Okay?" I sounded more exasperated than I was. "Meet me here tomorrow night around closing time?"

She looked away, and my stomach sank so far I figured I'd find it in the boiler room. "Please, just give me a chance here. I haven't let you down yet," I begged, hoping against hope she would look at me again.

She nodded and slipped off her stool. "I should get back to the office anyway," she said. I couldn't tell for sure how much I'd upset her, but she started building a wall, bricks forming around her with each step. At the door, she turned. "Tomorrow night, closing time." With those four words, the door closed behind her. I'd fucked up in some way I couldn't comprehend. I returned to the kitchen to check on Jonas.

He had pulled up a stool to his little kitchen counter and was making best friends with a chipped tumbler glass and a bottle of scotch. It would have sold for hundreds in the living world, but here it couldn't do anything but rot your gut. I intrinsically understood that kind of misery, so I focused on closing out business for the day.

I swept at debris that had probably been super glued to the ground, and wiped at sticky-spots on tables that had no intention of dissipating.

I returned shoes to their properly numbered slots, and placed bowling balls on racks according to weight. I dusted the lanes with a giant, unwieldy dust mop, and squeegeed in lane conditioner, so that even if the balls wouldn't knock every pin down, they'd at least make it to the end of the line. I switched the neon signs off, closed out the till in both registers, and went back to Jonas.

He'd passed out against the counter, one hand clasped around the rotgut scotch. I wrapped my arm around him and heaved him over my shoulder, nearly toppling the both of us in the process. Up the back stairs in the kitchen and a sharp turn to the right. I prodded the door to his apartment open with my foot. It was tiny, even smaller than mine.

I'd seen it a handful of times, but it still surprised me. I always thought that by virtue of seniority he'd have a somewhat nice place, but it made sense that he'd chosen this place for himself. The furnishings were beyond sparse—one sitting chair with a small pile of books, a kitchen table for one, with a gas stove in the corner, and a bed that could've been a cot. The only real thing of value hung on the wall next to his bed: a small golden frame housing an old black-and-white picture of a young couple. There was a handsome young man with a short cut and fair hair, holding hands with a beautiful young woman who held a passing resemblance to Mia.

As I laid him on his bed, covering him with the tattered excuse for a blanket, I hoped he'd see her soon.

I locked up the Depot and shivered out into the night, skipping past the train station and straying far from my apartment. I wandered down the sketchy back alleys that served as shortcuts on busy days, trying my best not to trip over my own laces, piles of trash, or lost souls sleeping. Somehow I managed to step in horse shit, though I couldn't recall seeing a horse once in twelve years.

I felt uncomfortably alone that night, the same way I had when I pressed the eject button on life. The discomfort wasn't enough to cripple me; my legs kept moving at a soldier's pace. But I could feel it constricting my brain, making me desperate.

I could tell Michael tomorrow "no deal," that I immediately wanted out of this awful place. Those thoughts nipped at my heels like angry dogs for six blocks. It was all I could do to follow through with my plan.

* * *

Down that alley, up on that wrought-iron terrace, he came off almost stoically, as if he were ruminating on some great mistake, but he seemed approachable, like any of the Archangels after you got over the initial shock. I felt sad for him. He looked just the same as he had a week before, and I assumed this has been his routine for centuries. He sat eating his applesauce from a tin, his bathrobe whipping in the wind, loose hair tangling around the stem of his spoon. As he pulled the spoon from his mouth, it glinted in the street light, hinting at an ornate design.

"I knew you'd be showing up," he said, his mouth full of mush.

"How?" I shivered, though I wasn't sure whether it was because of the temperature or his foresight. I was used to the angels being able to do it, but to my knowledge he was no angel.

He seemed amused. "I've been here longer than most. I know a great deal. And there aren't many courageous enough to visit," he muttered.

"You know, for something so powerful, you sure don't come off that way." I wasn't sure where my attitude was coming from, but I wasn't thrilled to be standing out in the frigid cold and playing a game of Dungeons and Dragons with some kook.

"I don't need to posture. Word of mouth spreads. Those around here know what I do. Most fear it. A few seek it out. I believe you fall in that latter category." He smiled, pulling down the hood of his bathrobe. I could see a rope burn around his throat, and his skin was ancient and sallow. He looked down the length of his crooked nose at me.

"So tell me who it is that requires my services. I know that you aren't here for yourself."

"How do you know that?" My hands were shaking in my pockets, all my preconceived notions escaping me. "Are you some kind of angel?"

"No," he laughed, his voice tinged with regret. "There are no wings under this robe, and there were never meant to be."

"So it's true then? You can do it?"

"For a price," he said. He pulled another can of applesauce from his pocket, snapping off the lid and tossing it to the alley below.

"I haven't got much," I said. Less than fifty dollars, and I wasn't getting paid well even before I was supposed to take the big trip upstairs.

"I don't ask for much," he chuckled, rubbing at the ring around his neck. "It's part of the rules. Thirty pieces of silver is the going rate." He sat his spoon down on the table, resting his chin and beard on his frail, spindly hands.

"I can handle that," I said, relieved.

"And you're sure that the recipient is okay with this? Once you pay me, the act will be done, one way or another. There are no refunds."

"Yes, absolutely. Just be at the Depot tomorrow, around closing time, please?" The words shivered out of me, as if the city streets around us had become a vast arctic wasteland. He gave a small nod and pulled his hood back over his head. Without another word, he returned to his applesauce.

He'd clearly tired of my company, so I turned my back to him, beginning the slow walk home. I couldn't shake the feeling that his eyes were on me until I was several blocks away. I wondered how much he knew about my plan, if it would even work, or if he was just some cosmic con-man with a spooky story and a weird affinity for applesauce. I worried about Mia, that she'd be upset that I'd planned this without her. But I was breaking her out of this place, and that had to mean something. I still wasn't even sure how I'd get him in the Depot without Jonas completely losing his little German mind. I just knew I had to do this. My mind raced the entire walk home, too busy overthinking every minute detail and scenario, every single possibility. This had to work.

15

Sleep was impossible that night. I'd grown accustomed to something I'd spent twelve years without, but the warmth and comfort of Mia was irreplaceable. Without her, everything seemed empty. I couldn't keep my eyes closed long enough to even attempt slumber. When the light finally drifted in through the cracked, dusty window, I crawled out of bed, neglecting to comb my hair and tucking in half my shirt as I buttoned my jeans. My socks didn't match, but they never did. They were all gray anyway.

I left the apartment determined to walk the length of the city to avoid the bus. I was done with that driver. The last thing I wanted was to play another game of snarky quips and guess-how-the-new-passenger-killed-themselves. I was too close to escape to deal with things like that. In the distance, the embarrassingly tall statue of St. Peter stood watch over his Courthouse like some vigilant emissary. He was my north star. I kept my head low, not wanting to observe the growing midday cacophony. Twelve years had been long enough, and this was it. This was escape, and happiness—what I'd been looking for long before I got here, and what I'd hopefully find when I left.

I stopped in a convenience store to acquire Michael's asking price. Everything was so unappealing, as though lingering depression from before was trickling in—a final cosmic "HA-HA gotcha!" before I pulled one over on the universe. Behind the counter at the convenience store stood the old Russian woman from the bus.

"Two packs of cigarettes," I said, holding two fingers up and avoiding eye contact.

"Any preference?" She did not have a Russian accent. I was taken aback, years of daydreaming slowly circling the drain with two words.

"Oh yeah. The red ones at the top," I said, pointing. I dropped exact change on the counter and hightailed it out of the store.

* * *

By the time I burst into Waiting Room 13, I was nearly out of breath but two minutes early. Janice looked at me like I was a bear snatching at the beehive on her head to extract every precious honeycomb.

"Excuse me!" that hoarse croak bellowed. "You're gonna have ta take a numb—"

"Nope." Michael's voice boomed in a way I'd not heard before. It was full of authority, a tone that would put the fear of God into anything. "He's my one o'clock. Come on back, kid." He gave me a friendly smile, then turned to Janice and glared at her in a way that could've melted steel.

Not one to argue with an Archangel, I shuffled past a full waiting room of unsavory looks. If those looks were a sundae,

Janice's malicious sneer was the fudge topping. I stepped carefully, avoiding the creaks I'd memorized over the years. In Michael's office, I plopped down into his cushiest armchair. It was a heavenly respite from the rest of the seating arrangements in this place.

"First things first," he growled, his usual greasy voice returning. "Them smokes."

I tossed the two packs onto his desk. He greedily ripped the cellophane from one pack like a kid opening his Christmas presents. He slid a cigarette between his lips, clicking his fingers twice before the bright red cherry appeared. Inhaling deeply, he kicked his feet back on his desk, ashing directly into the wastebasket. He sucked down the full cigarette in complete silence, his eyes fixed on the ceiling. Stubbing it out on the bottom of his loafer, he quickly lit another, and instead of relaxing again, brought his feet down to the floor, facing me directly.

The words came out with an unexpected force—a furious hurricane of admonishment.

"YOU BARELY KNOW THIS GIRL! DO YOU HAVE ANY IDEA WHAT THE ABSOLUTE FUCK YOU ARE DOING?! YOU ARE DISRUPTING THE NATURAL ORDER OF THINGS! DO YOU EVEN REALIZE THAT?! YOU WERE DOING SO GOOD!"

I slumped deep in the chair, somewhat of my own accord but mostly due to the heavy collision of his words. I thought maybe if I could just explain my line of thinking he'd get it.

"Well—"

He held his finger up to stop me, nearly inhaling the rest of his cigarette before continuing.

"Do you even know why she's here?" His question was a land mine I was too foolish to see.

"Well, I mean, no, she hasn't told me yet. But I'm sure she will. It takes some time—" And boom, there went my legs.

"No, Owen, it doesn't take time," he seethed, smoke barreling out of his nose as though the Archangel had himself become the serpent. "You know it the minute you get off the fucking train. You may take some time to process it, but it's always there in the back of your damn head."

"Okay, so she hasn't told me yet," I pleaded. "But like I said, I'm sure she will. She trusts me."

His sigh was angry and heavy and earthshaking. His cigarette-free hand extended toward his filing cabinet. Within seconds, a plain manila folder flew out, *Mia* written in red lettering on the tab. It landed wide open on his desk, right in front of me. I could see paragraphs and circles, names, dates, an obituary. But I didn't focus. I wouldn't let myself.

"All right kiddo, you don't wanna read it, I'll give you the summary." He put another cigarette in his mouth, this one lit without a single click of his fingers, as if it had kindled purely out of rage.

"Mia was a lot like you, kid. Smart, attractive, impressive. All the talent in the world." He grabbed yet another cigarette, tucking it behind his ear. "Things were a little bit different for her, though. She got sick, had a string of unhealthy relationships, some family trouble. School trouble. Trauma. Shit she couldn't forgive herself for. So while you found yourself a shower and a safety razor, she found herself a bridge. It's poetic, almost. Beautiful bridge in one of the prettiest cities in the world, looks like it's got salt-and-pepper shakers lined up along it."

He paused to inhale twice more as tears welled up in my eyes. I didn't want to know. "She used to walk the bridge at night, headphones in her ears, listening to music, looking for hope, for something to hold onto. You know what she found? Stray pieces of the bridge. Rocks, kid. She lost a younger sister, an awful accident that took place on her watch, and she never could let it go. Wasn't her fault, but she carried that with her like the weight of the fucking world. So she filled every pocket she had with every heavy thing she could find, shimmied her way around one of those pepper shakers, and jumped. You know why her eyes are so blue? Why she's goddamn pale? Why you can't help but smell sea salt around her and her hair always seems a little wet? She drowned, Owen. It all got to be too much, and she loaded herself down with rocks, just as heavy as the guilt, and she drowned. That's why she's here!"

I didn't want to believe him. I couldn't believe him. I followed the cherry of his cigarette as he pointed at the folder. I wish I hadn't watched. I'd have watched my own suicide a thousand times if it meant I never had to see this.

It was dark and she was surrounded by an incredible city. Bright lights shone in all directions. There was hardly any traffic, so I assumed it was early morning. She walked slowly but steadily across the bridge, in the same ragged jeans I'd cried into before, the same Thin Lizzy t-shirt I'd spotted the day we met. The shirt was covered in a dark-gray, hooded sweatshirt, the lettering on the front obscured by the straps of a backpack.

Her headphones were barely visible in her messy blonde lion's mane, but I faintly heard a song I recognized to be "A Case of You." I knew it well; Jonas occasionally played it on wistful nights in the Depot. It came from a small device in her pocket. She paced along the bridge and back twice, her feet quiet and lethargic. The song was on repeat the entire time. Occasionally I recognized her voice, softly singing along with Joni Mitchell. It was on her third go-round that things changed.

She stopped at one of the posts—or "shakers," as Michael had put it—and shimmied around to the side facing the water. I tried to look away, but Michael wouldn't allow it. She looked down into the water before dropping to her knees on the concrete. As she unzipped her backpack, I could see that it was full of stones. Some big, some small, some heavy, but all stone. She filled her pockets until they bulged, engorged with weight they were never meant to carry. The backpack hadn't even been half-emptied. She pulled it back over her shoulders, tying the loose straps together in as many knots as she could.

I heard the final notes of "A Case of You" play out one last time as one of the slender, caring hands I'd come to know and love made the sign of the cross over her body. And then she leapt. There was no grace, no hope, not even desperation. I shut my eyes tight as I heard the splash. Michael spared me the rest by closing the folder. It took me a moment to open my eyes. I tried desperately not to imagine her sinking into the water, her body thrashing as survival instincts kicked in.

It felt wrong, as if someone's diary had been forcibly read to me. I thought back on all of it, trying to piece together everything I knew, but I was completely gobsmacked—slumped in the chair, unwillingly sedated, tears streaking down my face.

"Why are you telling me all this, Mike? Why did you—" I felt useless, almost vegetative, and I couldn't speak. She understood how I felt more than I ever wanted her to. I needed to hold her and try to help, even if it was too late. I wanted to dive in and pull her out. To tell her that it would be okay. To help her stand up straight and find something in the night, in that great big city, that was greater than the pain she felt. But I couldn't move.

"The girl is a runner. She's a depressive, and she's a runner. She has a problem, she runs away from it. She finds a solution and runs away from that too. She finds reasons. Every time. She has to learn that sometimes what she needs really is right there for her. That's the lesson she's here to learn. Do you understand that? She has to learn that sometimes she fucks things up for herself and that sometimes you have to let go of guilt. All you're gonna do is help her run." His bark had cooled considerably, but he was still seething.

Those early fears of being her temporary solution came rushing back, filling me like a poisonous cloud. I felt violently ill.

"It's just like you. You're impulsive as all hell," Michael said. "One year in and you tried to break out. You meet this girl for all of fifteen minutes, and you're willing to stay here for her.

You fucking go and find the sin eater, of all people. Do you even realize who he is? And you concoct this plan to get you both out of here without even thinking about the rules you're bending, the fact that she's not getting anything out of this experience."

I hadn't been lectured like this in the In-Between. I wanted to curl into her lap, to hope that I meant something to her. That we were both capable of redemption.

"You know what, kid? I'm gonna do you a favor. You think you're ready to put your big-boy pants on? You want Paradise eternal for you and your girl?" He spat his words through his teeth, tearing open the second pack of cigarettes. "I'll give it to you. You tell her about your plan tonight, and if she goes through with it, you're both out of here, first thing tomorrow, front row seats up to Paradise." His arm stretched out and the cabinet drawer slid open. My file flew across the table and landed right next to hers.

The heat of his heavenly wrath was absolutely smothering. Someone had turned up the gravity in the room, and I was suffocating under his words and the weight they carried. I rubbed my scalp and dug through my pocket for something that could serve as a comforting distraction. No coins. No lighter. Nothing. I sat there, staring at a celestial being full of rage. I felt as if I'd disappointed a stepparent who just wanted to smoke cigarettes and talk to me about how cool the bands were when he was young.

"Either way, your ass is back in here tomorrow morning. Now get the hell out of here." Michael turned his back to me, his wings spreading as he pried open the blinds to peek at the gray sky outside.

I waited a moment, attempting to reassemble the pieces of me he'd expertly dismembered. Then I walked toward the door, face pallid, heart trembling, knees weak. I hit every damned creak in the hallway. Janice's taunting grin greeted me as I re-entered the waiting room.

I sat in the corner and waited for a while as lost souls filtered in and out through the door. I ignored all of them. All I could think about was what I'd seen, the weight of it hanging over me like a dark cloud of depression. No umbrella could ready me for the torrential downpour of angst and despair and empathy I felt for her. Now more than ever, I knew. I couldn't let her stay here. Not after that.

16

Somehow, I made it back to the Depot. I remember leaving
St. Peter's, and then I was sitting cross-legged on the
catwalk behind the lanes, trying to adjust the pinsetter
for Lane 12. The entire walk to work had passed by in a haze,
and I was coasting more than I had in the last days of my life.
I tightened screws haphazardly, knowing no one was going to
complain. Anyone who'd bowled a few frames at the Depot was
used to having pins set improperly or falling over.

I wiped the grease off on my jeans and glanced at the clock.
I could see Mia's blonde mane in her usual corner booth, so I
did my best to make myself presentable as I dashed down the
catwalk and over to her.

I took a shortcut through the kitchen, grabbing two clean
glasses from the racks and carrying them out to the counter to fill
them up. I couldn't show up at her table with such an important
proposition without drinks. As our glasses slowly filled, I tried
to think of the right approach.

"So," I said, sliding into the booth across from her. She'd

been chewing on the edge of her thumbnail, now nearly bare of its previous polish, and she looked up as I placed the glass of amber ale in front of her.

"So," she said back, watching as I pulled my sleeves down over my scars. "I looked into the Kennedy thing today when Uriel wasn't looking. Jonas was right. It was the CIA." Her smile was more reserved than usual.

"I told you. We all know that down here. It's usually the first thing people ask. Either that, or what happened to D.B. Cooper," I said.

"What happened to him?" Her eyes widened with excitement.

"Still alive, according to Michael. A fisherman in Maui. It's honestly kind of disappointing," I muttered, taking a sip of my beer.

"That is kind of disappointing," she said. "Speaking of, when were you going to tell me that you were leaving?"

I hadn't expected her to go in for the tough questions so early, but it was a fair point. I looked into my glass. "I don't know. Honestly. It was impulsive. I was supposed to leave when you got here, but I then saw you. I convinced Michael to let me stay, and I've really just been winging it, wracking my brain trying to figure out how I can just stay with you."

"Okay, I get that, but that still doesn't change the fact that, what, in a few days I'm going to have to find someone new to do this whole afterlife thing with?" I could see a little fire rising in her that I hadn't witnessed before.

"Well, what if we could both leave? Tomorrow."

"And how do you propose we do that?" She narrowed her eyes and took a sip of her beer. "Especially given that I'm supposed to be here for the next ten years."

I smiled. "The sin eater."

"The guy with the applesauce?"

"Well yeah, the guy with the applesauce," I said. My scars

started to itch. "But the fucking fruit doesn't matter. I talked to him last night. He's willing to do it for you. I've already got the money. He says a few things, eats something over you, takes a drink over you, and you're absolved. You're free. You're on the weekend train out of here."

"Right," she said. "No, I get how it works. But what about my lesson?"

"What about it?"

"Well, there's the fact that I haven't learned it? The fact that I haven't come to terms with how exactly I got here. We haven't even talked about it."

For the first time, I started to question myself.

"I know, I know, but Michael explained it to me. And I understand. I really do." I tried to be comforting and understanding, the way she had been for me when I broke down crying in her lap as Wolfman Jack howled about good times and dancing.

"What?" It was more cannon-shot than question. The fire from earlier was growing into the kind of all-consuming wildfire that levels forests and cities, as if I'd inadvertently committed an act of war.

"Michael explained—"

"Yes, I heard that. You listened? You let him? You let him tell you such a personal thing without even asking me?" Her eyes were imposing glaciers, and my hull was about to split open.

"Well, I mean, I didn't ask him to. He just kind of told me."

"Did he tell you everything? Did he tell you all about the family problems? Did he tell you how difficult it is to grow up the way I did? Did he tell you how awful Catholic school was? Did he tell you about the things I dealt with as a kid? Do you know what I lost?! Do you know any of that at all? NO? Then how the FUCK are you asking me to run away with you? How am I supposed to be okay with that, when you hardly even know me? When you're not even concerned with whether I find the penance I'm supposed to?"

"But, b-but . . ." I stammered. "He'll be here soon. I've already got the money for him. Can't you come to terms with all of that up there, rather than down here?" I didn't mean to be insensitive; if I could have frozen time and stepped outside of myself, I'd have given myself a good, hard punch in the face.

This was another one of those bullet points: big, bright, bold, and thoroughly heartbreaking. This was how I lost her.

She looked at me like I'd slapped her, and for a moment I thought the color drained from her eyes. She didn't finish her beer, didn't touch my hand, didn't leave her book behind. She tucked it under her arm, stood up, and walked toward the door. She didn't look back as I called her name, or turn as she opened the door. It was a silent goodbye, the sea breeze exiting the Depot as the door closed behind her. I finished both of our beers, still feeling like I needed a dozen more to slake this thirst.

I splintered into fragments as everything clicked into place. She was right. Of course she was right. I hadn't thought about anyone but myself. And Michael was right. I'd been completely and utterly impulsive. I wouldn't be leaving in two days; this was a bump in a long hard road that was not over yet. I had hurt one of the very few people in twelve years who truly cared about me. She hadn't even been here two weeks, and I'd already damaged her. I wasn't surprised she walked out the door, and I doubted she'd ever be back. It was over. My plan had been destroyed, and I'd proven myself to be an expert self-saboteur.

If it were possible, I would have ripped my arms open all over again, right there on one of the empty lanes.

17

As closing time neared, I stared at the door intently, wiping at scuffs on the counter that had been there for years. In a way, this exercise in futility was no different than throwing myself on the couch and devoting hours to *The People's Court*. Since our fight, the Depot had been dead. A lone lost soul turned in her ball and shoes after bowling two games on Lane 3. I spent two hours hoping Mia would walk back through that old wooden door and my luck would turn around. But it didn't. That wasn't the way this place worked, and this situation was no different.

Ten minutes before closing, a man walked in, bringing in a chill that felt all the worse because she wasn't here. His glasses sat delicately on his crooked nose, and his silver hair was cropped close to his head. I could see the faint outline of a long-weathered rope burn under his business suit. At least I knew how this one went, I thought as he stepped over to the counter, nary a scuff on his loafers. Jonas looked up at him warmly, as he always treated new faces.

"I am sorry, my friend," Jonas said, his spectacles sliding down his nose. "We're about to close up for the night. My assistant, he has already closed up the lanes."

"Oh, I'm terribly sorry," the man said. "It's been a very long day, friend, and I'm really just looking for a bite to eat. Could you do me that kindness?" I couldn't shake the nagging feeling that we'd met before. His voice had an almost-familiar tone, but I couldn't place him.

Jonas looked at me and shrugged. Looking back at the man and raising his hand, Jonas called him over. "Of course, of course, this is not a problem. But you will have to be the last meal of the evening. A man needs his sleep, after all."

The stranger walked toward the counter. His lips were so chapped I had to lick my own; they looked as if he'd spent his day avoiding water and kissing sandpaper. Jonas motioned me toward the door. I slid the lock and flipped the switch. The little neon train outside darkened to a halt.

"I have little left in the kitchen today, my friend," Jonas said, grabbing a glass from under the counter and filling it with a simple beer. "I hope that you do not mind, but your options are limited." He stopped, and a long, wrinkled finger pointed at the man in the suit. "I am sorry, my friend, but I did not ask your name. How terribly rude of me."

"Jude," the man said. He sat on a stool, crossing his arms in front of the beer. His smile was crooked but infectious, disarming.

"Ah, like the Saint," Jonas said, his froggy little hands clapping together.

Jude smiled. "There are no wings under this suit. These days, I like to think it's a bit more like the Beatles song." He checked his watch, which was silver and ornate and slightly scuffed, before returning his attention to my employer.

"Right on," I mumbled, lost in an awful valley of used and noxious shoes that not even a clown would consider fashionable.

"Wonderful. They were big in Germany, you know?" Jonas said. "But anyway, Jude, what can I get you this evening?" And then he stopped, chuckling. "Actually, it becomes more a question of, would you like some schnitzel and spiced apples?"

Jude laughed, his leathery hands resting on the untouched beer in front of him. "That sounds absolutely delightful, Mister—"

"*Ach*, my apologies, I have asked for your name and not given mine, how rude!" Jonas wiped his hands on his chest before extending one for a shake. "My name is Jonas Ehrlichmann. I am the proprietor here, and over there, the moppet with the shoes, that is my employee."

"Owen," I said as Jude's hand clasped with Jonas's. It was a warm handshake; I could feel it even from my kneeling position in front of the shoes. There was something binding about it.

As their hands separated, Jonas pushed his spectacles back up his nose, grabbed another glass and poured yet another beer. "Well then, as we are now friends, this is worthy of a toast." He raised his glass to Jude, who in turn raised his glass, sliding his arm under and around Jonas's.

"*Prost!*" Jonas exclaimed.

"*Prost,*" Jude repeated calmly, taking a sip of his beer as Jonas swallowed a good quarter of his own glass. Jude politely wiped at the corner of his dry lips, then turned his attention to the jukebox in the corner. He studied it carefully—the busted neon tubing, the kitschy wood paneling, the goddamned scrap of wallpaper that had sprouted in the lower left corner. "This will be a long shot, I'm sure. But your machine wouldn't happen to have a song called 'Escape,' would it?"

Jonas spun around, looking at his new friend like he'd just found his soulmate. "Do you happen to mean the one by Rupert Holmes? The song about piña coladas?"

"Ah yes, you know it?"

Jonas looked at me with impish delight and I sighed. The loud shuffling of my feet projected my objections. In front of the jukebox, I resigned myself to my fate, pulling out the silver coins that I'd intended to use for Mia's escape to play that goddamned song about running away.

"No, no. Owen!" Jonas called, peeking out from the nearby kitchen door. "This is on me. I would really like to hear it a few times tonight, and our new friend has requested it too. Put your money away. I will give you the code."

I looked at him, bewildered, but for the first time in hours I felt a smile starting to form. I wasn't sure what I had done, but I earned the code to the jukebox, the one privilege I hadn't earned in twelve years. I had tried to crack it in my spare time, but I wasn't sure the number of digits, and I was forced to make a list. Through sheer grit and determination, I made it all the way from single digits through 428. I gave up at that point. I had enough coins to play the songs I wanted to hear anyway. It would just be another great mystery of how this place worked.

But now, now I had earned it somehow.

"It is a long code. I know it by heart, but you may need to write it down," Jonas said, his eyes darting to make sure that our guest was not in earshot. He wasn't. Jude sat at the bar stool, smoking a cigarette from a golden pack like Uriel carried, watching the smoke billow up into the already stained ceiling. I was certain he was making shapes, but not concerned enough to focus on it.

"I'm ready, J, lay it on me," I said, my fingers wiggling, waiting to input this holy grail of numbers, even if it meant multiple plays of that goddamn pop song.

"*Eins, neun, zwei, null, neun, vier.*" Jonas whispered to me. "Did you get it?"

"One, nine, two, zero, nine, four," I repeated in a respectfully hushed tone.

"That is correct. 1920. 9 April. That was my Anneliese's birthday." It was one of the few times he'd said her name without tearing up. I was proud of him, and I felt honored to have both the code and the intimate knowledge he'd shared with me. I tapped it in without reservation, being careful not to dishonor him by miss-pressing. With reluctance, I tapped the *K*, followed by the *1* and the *3*. I did so multiple times, each more unpleasant than the last. I'd rather have gotten on my knees and started peeling away at that abyssal wallpaper. But Jonas was happy, and I didn't want to deny him that. Not when I'd managed to piss off half of the In-Between today. I wondered where Dante was shacking up and if maybe he'd like a roommate. I'm sure we could find some common ground; he liked books too.

I hated the song, but I couldn't help but raise my arms in the air. Though never a drummer in this life or any other, I could perfectly picture the movements. I air-drummed that opening beat like it could have saved my life, a little mini-catharsis as I floated in my sea of self-made bullshit. I turned to see Jude lightly tapping against his glass, still full save for the sip he'd taken with Jonas. He was smiling and bobbing his head slightly, the rope burn peeking out from beneath his collar. The more I looked, the more familiar he seemed, and the less I could place him. Perhaps he'd been a passenger on the bus. I'd seen so many these twelve years.

I left the jukebox, unenthusiastically resigned to the incoming repetition of the playlist, and made my way into the nearly empty café. I pulled a rag from my pocket and wiped at the tables, the booths, and the seats, sopping up liquid and knocking stray debris to the floor. Jude looked toward the kitchen door, waiting for Jonas to return. As I walked past again, I caught him humming along, the occasional lyric slipping between his chapped lips.

"*. . . if you're not into yoga . . . if you have half a brain.*"

I shook my head, walking into the backroom and returning with a broom and dustpan.

Halfway into the second playthrough of the classic, Jonas emerged from the kitchen smiling, his toes tapping that frog-step I'd known for so long. In his hands he held the cleanest plate we had, piled high with schnitzel and spiced apples. He presented the plate with great pride, setting it down in front of Jude and placing a knife and fork on either side of the plate.

"I assure you my friend, this will satisfy your appetite." His smile was bright, like the sparklers I'd lit on summer nights with my father, back before everything hurt so much.

Jude looked up at him gratefully. "Thank you, my friend," he said. He jabbed the tines of his fork into an apple.

Jonas reached out. "My apologies," he said, straightening the knot in Jude's tie. Jude didn't seem fazed; he simply lifted his arm higher to take a bite of the apple.

"To escape," he said, the apple slipping between his teeth. He chewed slowly, a smile rippling across his wrinkled cheeks. His skin seemed lighter. It was as if the slice of apple had rejuvenated him. Though he still looked weathered, his cheeks were less wrinkled, no longer bathed in a cold pallor. I could see warmth. The skin around his neck tightened, the rope burn looking less leathery. His lips remained dull and chapped, and no color returned to his hair, still argent and clinging softly to his scalp.

He placed the fork on his plate and looked up at Jonas, eyes twinkling. "I must confess, my friend, that may have been the best apple I have ever tasted, and I am quite the connoisseur." He looked down at his watch in a robotic, unconvincing manner. "Ah, but it is late. I've already kept you open after hours, and I've made you cook for me. I'm so very sorry, but I have an appointment this evening and I really must get to it."

Jonas looked confused, scanning for the words to say to his new friend, who seemed ready to abandon the nice little relationship they'd formed. Jude stood, pulling an ornate silver clip from inside his suit jacket. He removed two graying bills and placed them softly on the counter, nodding first toward Jonas with a smile, and then, strangely, to me.

"Goodbye, my friends," he said. "And Jonas, to you good luck. You are truly a wonderful man." With that he was gone, silently exiting through the door as quickly as he'd arrived. Somehow, I felt lighter, a feeling I couldn't explain. It wasn't that the cloud of melancholy had lifted, or that my heart hurt any less. Something was just . . . different.

"What a strange man," Jonas laughed, his eyes meeting mine. "Do you want to finish this?"

"I haven't got the stomach for it tonight, J, I'm sorry." I didn't think I'd be able to eat for weeks after the day I'd had. My stomach felt like it was full of angry ulcers, growling and gnashing and refusing me any sort of gastrointestinal peace.

He nodded, saying nothing as he grabbed the dishes on the counter and scuttled off to the kitchen. I punched Anneliese's birthday into the jukebox again, tapping out an old favorite on the keys. The selector arm picked an unmarked single, loaded it onto the platter, and as the needle plunked down, a familiar piano line plinked out. It wasn't one often heard in the Depot, but I remembered it from my childhood.

Whenever my father fought with my mother, he always return home from work with a dozen roses, roses she always said she hated, though she'd immediately place them in a vase and spend the next week working hard to keep them alive. Then he'd go to the shelf in the corner and pull out the same record. He'd set it on the turntable, playing it at a higher volume than I was ever allowed. He'd grab my mother by the hips, and for two and a half minutes he would slow dance with her to "Blueberry Hill," singing along softly with Fats Domino, just loud enough for her to hear. It was one of the few memories from before that ever really brought a smile to my face.

As I listened to Fats sing, I attended to the bowling ball racks, straightening them, organizing by weight, trying to separate by color, or at least shades of gray. I stepped back after every few placements, like an artist trying to make the perfect brush stroke. I wasn't sure how much time I wasted, but "Blueberry Hill" had long since ended. Stepping back to look at the nearly perfect monochromatic rainbow of polyurethane balls, I felt accomplished.

Before I left, I went into the kitchen to check on Jonas. I wanted to brag that I'd made a little art for in the morning. He peeked out from a crack in the door with an almost fatherly look.

"I know that today was not an easy day for you," he said, his stumpy arms wrapping around me. "But it will come with time. You will not be here forever, Owen."

I started to well up, tears trickling down my cheek to land on the shoulder of his cardigan. I thanked him before he could say anything else, returning the hug, the same way I'd have hugged my father.

We let go, and he laughed softly and told me it was far past his bedtime. As he hobbled up the back stairs, I told him I'd take care of the dishes and see him in the morning. I scraped Jude's scraps into the garbage can, dropping the plate and glasses into the sink. I scrubbed for hours.

Most days, I was resigned that nothing would ever come clean, but tonight I just had to try. I had to rid this plate of every smudge. I scrubbed with the dishrag until my hands began to prune, looking older than Jonas's, or even Jude's. When I pulled the plate out, a solitary smudge remained, directly in the middle. It was so goddamned disheartening. I put the plate in the drying rack and dried my hands on my jeans before grabbing the garbage from the can and leaving the Depot.

* * *

I took the long way home. I wasn't ready to see my shitty little apartment yet, the empty bed. I walked up and down city blocks, staying away from her side of the city. I felt unwelcome there, and I respected the fact that she'd probably rather drown all over again than hear from me right now. It might have been a few minutes, it might have been a few hours, but eventually I wound up in that sketchy alleyway, looking up at the sin eater's terrace.

"Hey!" I called up, my malaise manifesting as anger.

He didn't respond. He was there. I could see him. His long silver hair flowed in the night breeze from underneath his hood. His robe was as tattered as ever, pieces still wrapping around the wrought iron like malevolent tentacles. He was a deep, dark, vampire squid, existing only for his own nourishment, not concerned with anyone or anything. He could've been fused to that terrace like some hellish abomination. I wouldn't have been surprised to find that his bathrobe was lined with that awful art-deco wallpaper.

"HEY!" I yelled, not concerned with who might hear, who might notice the man I was interacting with.

He didn't look down, staring instead at the brick building across from him. His table was empty tonight; there were no empty tins of applesauce at his feet or in the alley below. I saw a twinkle in his eyes as they peeked out from beneath his hood, but his lips remained closed.

"HEY!" I yelled one more time, my voice a mix of desperation, fear, and pure pain.

Nothing. Not a single word. Not even an acknowledgement. I waited, hoping he'd have something to say. He didn't.

I walked home.

I traipsed up the stairs with the heaviest of feet, opening my apartment door with my shoulder and the slightest twist of the knob. I couldn't even make it to my bed, couldn't handle tugging at my clothes. It was too damn cold here anyway. I fell over the armrest on the couch and collapsed into a sleep that was deep but not at all restful.

18

I woke early the next morning, intending to run by the Depot before meeting with Michael. I had lucked out by not removing my clothes, I thought. I stared into the grimy, cracked mirror on my wall. I felt weathered, but I didn't look any older. I hadn't aged a day in twelve years. The bags under my eyes were still there, but there were no new wrinkles, no thinning or graying hair, nothing.

I picked at my hair before settling on my inability to do anything presentable with it, then looked around for my keys. My wallet was still in my pocket, but all my coins had disappeared. They'd probably fallen into the hole in my couch, a hole that had devoured countless books, socks, and various other goods. I didn't have the energy to concern myself with missing change, so I snatched my keys off the floor by the door and left. I caught myself humming "Escape" as I tottered down the steps, and I rolled my eyes.

As I passed the train station—grand and magnificent, its steam rising into the great big monochrome—I didn't turn my head to look. I wasn't concerned with the new arrivals; their fresh faces and wide-eyed confusion; that brief moment when they realized there were no language barriers and they all understood one another. And I certainly didn't want to see who was leaving. I couldn't bring myself to think about my failed attempt at an escape plan, the kind of "Born to Run" that would have disappointed Springsteen himself. Fortunately, I could see the Depot up ahead, and it was calling to me like a beacon.

It was locked, which threw me off a bit. I could understand the neon sign not beaming out into the morning sky, but Jonas was the early-to-bed, early-to-rise type. I assumed he'd forgotten as I fidgeted with my keys.

I turned the knob and stepped into relative darkness. Confused, I flipped on the lights and went behind the counter. Nothing seemed out of place.

"Jonas? Where are you, buddy?" I called, setting my keys next to the register. I scanned the lanes, peeking into the kitchen to see if he was whipping up a pastry or mopping back and forth like he habitually did. Nothing.

I ran down a lane and opened the door leading to the catwalks. Maybe the old man decided to tinker with the pinsetters? He'd been saying he was convinced that he could get Lane 3 to function properly again. But he wasn't there, and I started to get nervous.

I closed the door to the catwalk, breaking into a sprint up the lanes, nearly tripping over my own laces as I made my way into the kitchen and up the stairs to his little room. The door was shut.

I let myself breathe, finally, air flooding my lungs in relief. He was probably just in bed, sick. It wasn't as if you could die here—not as far as I knew anyway—but he could've come down with a cold. I gave a quick, sharp knock.

"Hey Jonas? It's Owen, man. Can I come in?"

Nothing. I waited for a brief moment before knocking again.

"Jonas. Hey, come on. Our day's about to start. I have to meet with Michael and you've got to get this place up and running."

Still nothing. I pressed my ear to the door, cupping my hands, listening for any sign of activity. There was no rustling of sheets or shuffling feet. No wheezing, coughing, sneezing, heavy breathing, or groaning. So I opened the door.

The apartment was nearly empty. The bed had been neatly made, the ratty old sheets pressed, the sorry excuse for a pillow fluffed. The picture of Jonas and Anneliese had disappeared from the wall. His closets were empty, along with his cupboards, his sink. Aside from the standard-issue furniture, there remained two items, both neatly arranged on his tiny kitchen table.

I pulled the lone chair out and sat down calmly. A large, dusty notebook sat in front of me, *Recipes* written across it in Jonas's precise script. The other object was a sealed envelope on which he had written my name.

I sat for a moment, not quite sure what to say or think. I picked up the letter. The weight of it was crushing, as if it carried heavy burden and purpose. I slid my finger along the flap, pulling out a single notebook page.

Like always, his penmanship was impressive.

Owen,

It seems that today we both received an unexpected promotion. Gabriel phoned me early this morning and asked me to come down to the courthouse. He insisted that I have my affairs in order before doing so. When I arrived, he took me into his office and we spoke of my time here—how long I had stayed, unable to forgive myself for the things that I had done in my life. We talked about my guilt and fear, of facing my Anneliese, meeting my child Monika. I did so many horrible things, but Gabriel reminded me that I am not a bad man. For the first time, I believed him. When I woke this morning, I felt lighter, a great burden relieved from me. It is not something that I can explain, but I am ready.

Gabriel even showed them to me. I cannot begin to tell you how I wept, watching how happy they seemed. My daughter is the most beautiful thing I have ever seen, my Annaliese just as enchanting as the day I left on that train. By the time you read this letter, I will sit on a different train, one that will carry me toward my family, not away from them.

I would like for you to know that you have been a wonderful employee. Even when you were lazy with your mopping or bad with the dishes, you did as I asked, and you treated me with respect. This is something I cannot truly repay. I have no possessions here, just this bowling alley and these recipes. So I will leave them with you, and though I hope that you do not have to use them for a long time, I believe they will at least carry you through until you cross over as well. It is now my great hope that I will see you again soon.

Good luck with your penance, with your sea girl, and with the Depot.

Regards,

Jonas Ehrlichmann

His signature was smudged a bit. I wasn't sure whether from my tears or his.

I stood up and walked over to the wall, grabbing the nail that previously kept his picture frame hanging. I gave it a hard tug, and then another before it came loose, little bits of sheet rock tumbling behind it. I held the letter up over the freshly uncovered hole and inserted the nail. That would do for now.

Returning to the table, I grabbed the recipe book and thumbed through it, fascinated. Each recipe I'd seen Jonas prepare was written out with precise measurements and strict steps. He'd left notes in the margins—little additions he'd added over the years, jukebox selections he liked, even thoughts on customers. Michael was listed as *SCHMUCK*, the word underlined four times.

It occurred to me that if I sat there any longer, I'd miss my designated appointment and tongue-lashing. I brought the recipe book down to the kitchen, ripped a blank page from the back, and wrote *DEPOT TEMPORARILY CLOSED* in big bold lettering, taping it to the ancient front door. As I left the Depot, I locked the door, not yet grasping that I'd be fully in charge when I got back. We were at least going to change some of the songs in that jukebox, even if I had to petition one of the saints. Was a Stones single so much to ask for?

I hustled toward the center of the city, prepared to take my medicine. I knew Michael was not going to be happy with me, with what I'd done. But at the same time, I couldn't be too angry with myself. Sure, I fucked up what I thought was an incredible opportunity with the most beguiling and intriguing woman I'd ever met. I'd run the risk of her never speaking to me again, and that was an especially disquieting thought, knowing that there was an afterlife that stretched on for all of eternity.

But, I thought, maybe I hadn't lost those silver coins in the couch. Maybe the services I'd asked for had indeed been rendered, by a man in a charming disguise, for the person In-Between who probably deserved it most. That thought allowed me to keep my head up. I did my best to avoid the other foot traffic, but my shoulder managed to snag the arm of a man in a business suit. The same one who'd held up my bus two weeks prior by refusing to pay bus fare for some mundane reason. He grimaced, as if my touch were toxic, like the plaid of my shirt would eat away at his fine silk jacket. I wondered if he might rip it off, thinking it forever tainted.

"Watch the hell out, kid!" he screamed, one pointed strand of his slicked-back hair flying forward as if challenging me to a duel.

I didn't even stop. I kept my hands buried in my pockets, both middle fingers firmly resting next to their fellow appendanges, all the vulgarities floating around in my head quietly filed away for later use. It just wasn't worth my time.

As I crossed the street in front of the courthouse, I felt something unexplainable. It wasn't joy or triumph, tedium or ennui. It wasn't disappointment or deflation; it wasn't even resignation. I just had to do this. It became a sort of mantra as I took every step slowly and confidently. It guided me as I pushed past the crowd, past the giant excess of St. Peter. It helped as I used every ounce of strength to muster open those heavy wooden doors. It shepherded me to Waiting Room 13—through the crowds, the old hands, the new blood, the angels looking up at the large clock above the doorway, anxiously waiting to punch out for the day and return to their astral lofts in the skies above, or wherever the hell Paradise happened to be. When I opened the door, I felt a surprising comfort.

"NUM-bah. Take one," Janice belched, her beehived head tilting so far toward the ticket machine that I thought it might roll right off, plopping to the floor, somehow still sentient and ready to bark her stock phrases as her hands idly clicked away at a keyboard. I did as I was told. I was lucky enough to pull a six, but I wasn't sure how lucky that really was in a waiting room full of twenty.

I sat next to a big, burly man. The top of his head was completely smooth, his legs as thick as barrels, and his arms might've actually been two tree trunks. I imagined him as a career criminal, the kind of guy you would bring with you to shake someone down when they owed you more than a couple of dollars; or maybe some circus strongman, the kind that put on a tiger-striped toga and wrestled with a bear.

To kill the time, I tried to make conversation. "Are you new?" I asked, looking up at him.

"First week," he said. "Supposed to get my job assignment today. Michael said he might have something that fit my expertise."

"Oh yeah?" I laughed. "I don't know that we need a lot of human wrecking balls down here."

"Right," he said, giving me a slanted look. "Well, I'm actually a mechanic. Used to work on pinsetters in a bowling alley."

A disbelieving smile cracked across my face while laughter erupted from the depths of my belly. He looked puzzled, and I gathered stares from around the room, some of my fellow waiting-room compatriots no doubt assuming I was a lunatic. I calmed myself quickly enough and extended my hand toward him.

"I'm Owen, man, and believe it or not, I've got a bowling alley with some messed up lanes."

"Jackson." His hand nearly crushed mine like a walnut as he grasped and shook.

"I've got a feeling that you and I are going to—"

"SIX! NUMBAH SIX!" Janice was a hoarse and horrible alarm clock.

"Sorry, man. That's my number," I said, standing. "But I think we might be seeing each other later."

I walked past him, past the rest of the lost souls who leered at me as if I were a child cutting in front of the lunch line to get the last ice cream bar.

"Remem-bah," Janice started, her sandpaper-shredded vocal chords ready to warble out her normal speech.

"Yes. I've heard it all before, Janice. End of the hall, door to the left, don't open the one on the right."

She briefly looked at me with what seemed to be complete and utter defeat, as if I'd fractured her very purpose for being. I could almost see whatever soul she might have shatter into a thousand little slivers. Then she shrugged and went back to clacking away at her keyboard.

I walked down the hallway without a pack of cigarettes for the first time since the first time. I stopped at Michael's door, as I'd always done, and considered what might happen if I checked behind the door on the other side. But I had things to do. Amends to be made. I opened Michael's door and stepped in, waiting for whatever fury he might have.

He was seated at his desk, his feet propped up on the table, his wings extended at odd angles—one half-hidden by a potted fern, the other set on tangling with his blinds like Christmas lights. He held a book. It was small and blue, with a bright pair of eyes and an elegant title on the cover. I noticed the grease smudge on the back, my thumbprint. It was, without question, the copy Mia had given me.

"Not a bad book," he chuckled, closing it and setting it on the desk. "Owen, how about you take a seat?"

I sank into his plush armchair, watching as he straightened up in his own office chair, rolling his sleeves up and bringing his hands together to rest his mouth on them. I couldn't tell if he was waiting for me to explain myself or if he was trying to conjure the proper words with which to whip and flay me. We sat in silence for a few moments, him staring intently at me, me rearranging myself in the seat across from him. By the time he spoke, my posture was nearly perfect.

"That was a hell of a stunt you pulled," he said. His voice was calm, even a little jovial. Familiar.

"Yeah," I said, doing my best to take ownership of what I'd done. "It was my mistake, and I recognize that."

"Well, it was only about half your mistake," he said, pulling at the packet of cigarettes in his breast pocket. "I kind of set you up for failure on that one."

I tried to process what he could possibly mean.

"I hated to have to do it to you kid, but it was kind of a two birds, one stone thing," he said. He lifted the pack to his lips and removed a cigarette. It took him three clicks to get it burning brightly. "Look, Jonas was a real class act, but he was a glutton for punishment. He deserved his happiness. He'd have spent the rest of time here trying to atone, and the guy was in the clear well before you even came along. But we couldn't make him go. I can't take anyone's sin away. I don't have the power of absolution. And you." He took a long drag off his cigarette and looked away from me, unhappy with what he was about to say. "You weren't really ready to go. And I'm not happy about that kid. I'm not mad at you. I get it, this place isn't easy. It's not any easier than it is when you're living. But you were coming down to the wire and something was missing."

I stared ahead, the pieces slowly coming together in my head. Leaning forward, my elbows found support on his desk, and I cradled my chin in my palm.

"You were here not just because you killed yourself, and you know that. Nobody can hold that against you, not me, not God, not anyone. But you were impulsive. Thoughtlessly so. Even here. A little impulse is good, but it has to be balanced." He took another long drag, exhaling toward the window as he ashed into an ornate goblet on his desk. "And I'm not saying you were wrong with Mia, that there isn't something there. But this is eternity. Your time here isn't quite as fleeting as it is on earth. Eventually, you two would've come around to each other."

He ashed his cigarette again before pointing at my file.

"It's all in there, kid. Everything that has happened or will happen, from your conception all the way to the end, when eternity blinks out and we're all just stardust. You want to know what happens between you two? Go ahead and look. Page fifteen." He pushed the folder toward me.

I lifted my head. There was my name in big, bold red lettering. I placed my hand on it and it felt warm, as if this manila folder contained a piece of my soul, my very essence. My fingers crept along the cover, skittering toward the edge, eager to look inside. To know.

I slid the folder back across the desk. The Archangel smiled at the gesture. I'd at least managed to pass this little test.

"All right kid. So that's that. Get your shit out of your old apartment, we're putting you in the bowling alley now. I think you've met Jackson, right? He'll be showing up there later. Guy's built like a fucking brick house, right? But he's got a mind for mechanics. Probably won't help them pin machines you got, but hey, it ain't always easy finding a use for these cats." He took one last drag of his cigarette. "We're adding a little more time to your sentence, but I think we might have you squared away. Now. Before I kick you out so you can get them lanes up and running, you got any questions?"

A million. I had a million questions. I wanted to know everything he could possibly tell me. I wanted to know if I'd see her again. I wanted to know if Jonas had already gotten to his family. I wanted to know about my family. I wanted to know if I could have just a tiny peek into that folder without tacking on more time. I looked down, noticing for the first time that my scars didn't seem so pronounced, as if someone had ever so slightly washed them away, just enough that I'd notice.

"Just one," I said, standing. "What the hell's behind that door on the right?" I nodded backward to the twelve-year taboo across the hall.

"Elevator, kid," he chuckled. "That's how I get home every day. I hate trains. Way too crowded."

I just shook my head and smiled, taking it all in—the past two weeks, how hard and how far I'd fallen, how I'd basically been used as a cosmic tool, and in a way, she had too. I wondered if that was the way it really worked around here. If it was closer to real life than they let on, and if we were all just fumbling and fucking and fighting our way to being the people that we're meant to be.

I waved, telling Michael I'd see him in a couple weeks. I wasn't sure how much longer I'd be staying here. I didn't know if I'd ever see Mia again, but I understood that it wasn't my place to save her. I didn't expect to even be afforded the opportunity. I didn't know how I'd get by without Jonas to talk to, but Jackson would probably make it a little easier. All at once, I felt just as lost as I was on my first day, and yet I was playing with a full deck. Michael smirked knowingly, lighting one more cigarette.

And then I left his office, closing the door behind me. I took a moment to lean against it, looking across the hallway at Michael's escape route, a way out. It didn't even seem to have a lock on it. I could've escaped on the very first day. I could've run away with her the day she got here. I could've left right then and there. Instead, I walked down the hallway, out of the waiting room, through the courthouse, and out into the In-Between.

Epilogue

Light shone through the lone window, directly onto my face. I kept promising myself that I'd move the damn bed, but that was a lie. I stumbled out of from under the covers and across the floor, shuffling into the kitchen just long enough to put the kettle on. I yawned loudly and left the kitchen for the bathroom, where I took a piss that might actually have qualified for legendary. I wasn't truly awake until I noticed, mid-stream of course, the gaudy wallpaper spreading like mold from the bottom corner of the wall. Just another thing I'd have to add to my to-do list. I washed my hands, remembering that it was Wednesday and that Uriel always visited for lunch on Wednesdays. If I complained, maybe she could get one of those cleaning crews in here.

I wandered back into the kitchen just in time for the kettle to howl, a sound far too shrill for this early in the day. I poured the water into my mug and steeped my tea for longer than normal. It wasn't that I liked it that way, or even that I liked it at all. The taste was still horrendous, and I'd have been much happier to drink the beer from tap four downstairs, but the tea comforted me. It reminded me of that night, nearly nine months ago, when I confessed to the girl how I'd gone. When I finally came to terms with it. The tea wasn't her kiss, but it was all I had. I hadn't seen her since the night before Jonas left. The night I ruined it. I tried not to dwell as I waited for my tea to cool, blowing at the steam as I shuffled around the little apartment that I'd inherited.

I sipped the tea as I started gathering clothes—tugging at jeans, throwing on a plaid work shirt, affixing my nametag. I spilled the last bit on my denim while attempting to balance the mug on my knee and tie my boot laces. It was always something. I just let a small sigh slip out and placed the mug in the sink, wiping at the spot on my jeans with a mostly dry dishrag.

Finally, I was ready to greet the working day, and I wandered down into the kitchen of the Depot. Jackson was already there, pulling pastries out of the oven like a barrel-chested baking wizard. He nodded at me as I descended. I'd grown fond of him over the past nine months. He hadn't been quite as exciting as Jonas, but he was stimulating enough all the same.

He died tragically in the real world, a car wreck just as he was turning his life around. He'd been a deadbeat dad, and during his first few months he was very resentful of himself. I gave him free reign to help me run the Depot, and it impacted him tremendously. We were both surprised at how naturally responsibility came to him. He'd open earlier in the mornings, and I'd close later in the nights. We didn't run as tight a ship as Jonas had, but we maintained our steady stream of lost souls looking for decent food and broken games of tenpin.

"You sleep okay, pal?" he asked, placing his tray on the counter. He carefully grabbed each hot pastry, dropping them quickly onto a serving tray. I wondered if his calloused fingers even felt the burn.

"Yeah, man. A couple of bad dreams, but I'm alive and well . . . err . . . dead and well, I guess." I shrugged. "Nice looking pastries."

"Hey, man, thanks. That recipe book is pretty easy to follow. That Jonas guy knew what he was doing. You want one?" He extended the tray toward me, but I politely declined.

"I'm gonna go ahead and turn the lights on. Let's get the day started so we can get it over with." I smirked and walked past him out into the Depot. Even in the dark, it felt like home, and there was something about flicking the light switch in the morning that was invigorating, as if in some small way I was giving life to something.

I flicked each switch with practiced precision—first the main lights, then the café lights, the main power to the lanes, and finally, the outside lights. The routine was always punctuated with a twist of the lock, and then I scuffled over to the jukebox. I thought sometimes that maybe I'd picked up Jonas's little frog-man step, but that may have been nostalgia—or wishful thinking.

* * *

Most days were slow to start. Nothing ever picked up until lunch, but by then Jackson and I were in perfect tandem. He was the Keith to my Mick, expertly whipping food out from the kitchen as I dashed food to customers, ringing up customers for a couple of frames while I dug out the perfect pair of shoes and turned on the scoreboards. Sometimes, in the rush of everything, I was almost certain that I caught faint hints of it, that saltwater sea-breeze smell, but she was nowhere around. For a long time after she left, I wondered if that scent was just natural to her, or if it was just something that stuck with all of the drowned, a signature like my scars. From what I could gather, they only carried a similar pallor and glassy eyes, and theirs were never quite like hers. I didn't think that was even possible.

It was almost ironic. I'd been dead for just around thirteen years, and here I was, being haunted by the ghost of a girl who had changed everything, my entire afterlife.

I was always relieved to see the lunch crowd die down, because it afforded me a chance at the jukebox again. I pressed in the code that had meant so much to Jonas, one that I'd purposely neglected to share with Jackson, and in his honor, I punched in a *K*, followed by the inevitable *1* and *3*.

I was happy to hear the drums and synth kick in, but I was elated to hear the voice behind me. It was dry but wise, tinged with just a bite of cynicism.

"You know," Uriel called to me, "I thought when he left you'd never play this damn song again." I turned around, all smiles for the Archangel and her messy bun. She greeted me with a grin warmer than her voice had ever sounded. I was proud to elicit such a reaction in her. I felt nearly as close to her as I did Michael.

"What's the matter Uri, don't like piña coladas?" I laughed, moving behind the counter to grab her a menu.

"Of course I do, I just don't like bad music," she snarked back before plopping down on one of the stools at the café counter. "And you know I don't need one of those menus either."

"Right, fair point," I said, elbows propped against the counter. Kicking my foot backward against the kitchen door, I called to Jackson that I'd need an order of *Jägerschnitzel*. I listened for the affirmative grunt from my brawny partner before closing the door and turning back to her heavenly presence. I pulled a glass from under the counter to pour her the usual. "Oh, hey, while I've got you here. There's some of that wallpaper growing in my bathroom upstairs."

Uriel tensed up, her wings quickly stretching to their full span before shrinking inward again as color rushed to her cheeks. She plunged a hand deep into her shoulder bag and removed a small, leather-bound black notebook and a silver ball-point pen. She flipped the cover open, frantically turning pages until she found what I assumed to be a blank one, where she furiously scribbled the information that I'd given her, stopping only briefly to leer at her pen.

"Fucking thing is running out of ink," she mumbled angrily.

"No rush or anything, just, when you can get around to it," I said, trying to calm her down. She didn't respond, instead flipping forward a few pages in her notebook, scratching things out and making notations in the margins. I idly counted coins in the till as she attended to her business.

"Owen."

Thirty-seven big silver pieces.

"Owen"

Forty-two little silver pieces.

"Owen."

"What?" I looked up from the register to see the Archangel staring at me, annoyed. I rubbed the back of my scalp out of nervous habit as I replied, "Sorry Uri, I got lost a little bit there."

"It's fine," she replied, a note of frustration wrapped like a bow around the terse phrase. I knew what she wanted almost immediately, so I turned my back on her and peered through the kitchen door at Jackson. He stood in front of the stove, dwarfing it like a cartoon gorilla, frantically shaking a cast iron skillet back and forth. I could hear the grease splattering, and I laughed to myself as he recoiled like a small child, rubbing at his arm like he'd dipped it into a vat of molten iron. I closed the door quietly to spare his feelings and returned to my guest.

"It looks like it's going to be a few more minutes," I shrugged, pulling a golden pack of cigarettes from under the counter and offering one. She happily accepted, lighting the cherry with a quick snap of her fingers and sucking down the first drag, the furrow in her brow relaxing. "He hasn't quite taken to everything in the recipe book yet, and we don't get a lot of orders for *Jägerschnitzel*. Hey, speaking of, how is the old man?"

Uriel returned to her shoulder bag, her arm somehow disappearing, reaching far deeper than should have been possible. She clenched the cigarette between her lips, and her eyes rose to the ceiling as she strained for something in that cosmic bag of wonder. A small *hmmm* clued me in that she'd found what she was looking for, and after an absurd amount of pulling, her arm emerged from the bag with a picture that I somewhat recognized.

It was in a familiar, small golden frame, but the picture had changed. The handsome young man with the short, fair hair was still there, though his smile was bigger than I remembered. Sitting next to him was the beautiful young woman from before, but they were no longer holding hands. In her arms she was cradling a young girl in a dress, with curly wisps of blonde hair and a smile that could only have come from Jonas himself.

"I—how—is this?"

"This is a few weeks ago," she said, sliding the frame across the counter and into my hands. "Jonas thought you might like to have it." She wasn't smiling, but her expression was warm and understanding.

"But how—he's so young?"

"Things are different up there. You'll learn that soon enough." She rested her forearms on the edge of the bar, smoke trailing from the cigarette held between her fingers. "Word on the street is, you haven't got much time left."

"I don't know about that," I shrugged. "Michael's keeping his cards pretty close to his chest on that one." I glanced back at the photo, happy that Jonas had finally gotten what he deserved, and that he finally had the chance to make up for lost time with his wife and daughter. But looking at the picture for too long gave me an uncomfortable, queasy feeling. The similarity between Anneliese and the girl I'd known was unshakable. It wasn't necessarily the eyes or the smile, it was just this unnamable quality, some inherent warmth hiding in her frame. I slid the photo under the counter before my mind could wander too far. "Thank you for this."

Uriel nodded agreeably, puffing on her cigarette like she was trying to resuscitate it. "So how about that food, Owen?"

I rolled my eyes before pivoting and prodding my head through the kitchen door once more. Jackson had just lifted the cutlet onto the plate, delicately moving it so that it sat at the perfect angle. He lifted a pot from the stove, carefully ladling out a creamy, brown sauce, making sure not to ruin his perfect image. I once again pivoted, eyes rolling even harder this time.

"It's coming. I swear, you're the only one that ever orders it. You may be the only person who ever sat at this counter that actually enjoyed it," I chuckled, grabbing a rag from underneath the counter and wiping down the spot next to her.

"Mia didn't mind it," she replied blankly, taking another relaxed drag on her cigarette, as if she hadn't just taken that flaming sabre of hers and cleaved my heart in two. This was the first mention of Mia's name since that day in Michael's office. Even when I told Jackson the entire story of what had happened—the first meeting, the work time wasted sitting across from her in the corner booth, the junkyard, the escape plan, and my one big fuck up—I managed to do it without saying her name.

For nine months, I'd locked those three letters in the back of my mind and refused under any circumstances to let them escape and take that shape. I looked at Uriel, my eyes scrunched, my mouth agape, the corners drooping. Uriel straightened up as she noticed my devastation.

"She still asks about you, for what it's worth." It came across as sincere and not just an attempt at placating me, but my mind was already racing, desperately searching for a response that I knew I wouldn't find.

I nodded at Uriel, thanking her, before opening the kitchen door. Jackson arrived with her food, and once again pork cutlets got me out of an uncomfortable situation. I dipped through the swinging door before it could close, and sidled up to the sink and the murky water it contained.

Like my predecessor, I dropped my hands in and began scrubbing, plate after plate, glass after glass. Nothing came perfectly clean. That was the nature of this place. But even with chips in the glasses and cracks in the porcelain of the plates, they were still perfectly good and useable, maybe even charming in their own way. The damage wasn't damning; it was just a mar on something perfectly useable.

I washed nearly every dish in the kitchen, keeping my hands in the water until they pruned, long after Jackson said his goodnights and locked up for the evening. For a moment, I was certain that I smelled that saltwater sea breeze, though I knew that she wouldn't be there when I turned around.

I slept well that night.

Acknowledgments

Thank you to John Köehler, Joe Coccaro, Hannah Woodlan and the rest of the team at Köehler Books for the incredible opportunity, the belief in this book, and for making it so much easier than my anxiety led me to believe was possible. To Richard Rowland, thank you for the leg up, the guidance, and taking a chance on a manuscript completely out of left field. A big thanks to Amy Tober, for providing a helping hand in German and Brittany Morris for the amazing artwork and design ideas she's given me along the way. Thank you to Jeffery Everett for the incredible cover art and taking a chance on a kid with a dream. To Jen Mueller, a gigantic, eternal thank you for being the best front-line editor a fella could ever ask for, and polishing a sad Catholic rock and roll story into a diamond. Last but not least, thank you to Tyler Henry for picking me up and pushing me toward the finish line, and to my parents for supporting me through this, and every other, endeavor.